BLACK EDGE

CHARLOTTE BYRD

BYRD BOOKS

ABOUT BLACK EDGE

I don't belong here.

I'm in way over my head. But I have debts to pay.

They call my name. The spotlight is on. **The auction starts.**

Mr. Black is the highest bidder. He's dark, rich, and powerful. He likes to play games.

The only rule is there are no rules.

But it's just one night.

What's the worst that can happen?

PRAISE FOR CHARLOTTE BYRD

"Decadent, delicious, & dangerously addictive!" - Amazon Review ★★★★★

"Titillation so masterfully woven, no reader can resist its pull. A MUST-BUY!" - Bobbi Koe, Amazon Review ★★★★★

"Captivating!" - Crystal Jones, Amazon Review ★★★★★

"Exciting, intense, sensual" - Rock, Amazon Reviewer ★★★★★

"Sexy, secretive, pulsating chemistry..." - Mrs. K, Amazon Reviewer ★★★★★

"Charlotte Byrd is a brilliant writer. I've read loads and I've laughed and cried. She writes a balanced book with brilliant characters. Well done!" -Amazon Review ★★★★★

"Fast-paced, dark, addictive, and compelling" - Amazon Reviewer ★★★★★

"Hot, steamy, and a great storyline." - Christine Reese ★★★★★

"My oh my....Charlotte has made me a fan for life." - JJ, Amazon Reviewer ★★★★★

"The tension and chemistry is at five alarm level." - Sharon, Amazon reviewer ★★★★★

"Hot, sexy, intriguing journey of Elli and Mr. Aiden Black. - Robin Langelier ★★★★★

"Wow. Just wow. Charlotte Byrd leaves me speechless and humble... It definitely kept me on the edge of my seat. Once you pick it up, you won't put it down." - Amazon Review ★★★★★

"Sexy, steamy and captivating!" - Charmaine, Amazon Reviewer ★★★★★

" Intrigue, lust, and great characters...what more could you ask for?!" - Dragonfly Lady ★★★★★

"An awesome book. Extremely entertaining, captivating and interesting sexy read. I could not put it down." - Kim F, Amazon Reviewer ★★★★★

"Just the absolute best story. Everything I like to read about and more. Such a great story I will read again and again. A keeper!!" - Wendy Ballard ★★★★★

"It had the perfect amount of twists and turns. I instantaneously bonded with the heroine and of course Mr. Black. YUM. It's sexy, it's sassy, it's steamy. It's everything." - Khardine Gray, Bestselling Romance Author ★★★★★

BLACK EDGE SERIES READING ORDER

1. Black Edge
    2. Black Rules
    3. Black Bounds
    4. Black Contract
    5. Black Limit

CHAPTER 1- ELLIE

WHEN THE INVITATION ARRIVES…

"*H*ere it is! Here it is!" my roommate Caroline yells at the top of her lungs as she runs into my room.

We were friends all through Yale and we moved to New York together after graduation.

Even though I've known Caroline for what feels like a million years, I am still shocked by the exuberance of her voice. It's quite loud given the smallness of her body.

Caroline is one of those super skinny girls who can eat pretty much anything without gaining a pound.

Unfortunately, I am not that talented. In fact, my body seems to have the opposite gift. I can eat nothing but vegetables for a week straight, eat one slice of pizza, and gain a pound.

"What is it?" I ask, forcing myself to sit up.

It's noon and I'm still in bed.

My mother thinks I'm depressed and wants me to see her shrink.

She might be right, but I can't fathom the strength.

"The invitation!" Caroline says jumping in bed next to me.

I stare at her blankly.

And then suddenly it hits me.

This must be *the* invitation.

"You mean…it's…"

"Yes!" she screams and hugs me with excitement.

"Oh my God!" She gasps for air and pulls away from me almost as quickly.

"Hey, you know I didn't brush my teeth yet," I say turning my face away from hers.

"Well, what are you waiting for? Go brush them," she instructs.

Begrudgingly, I make my way to the bathroom.

We have been waiting for this invitation for some time now.

And by we, I mean Caroline.

I've just been playing along, pretending to care, not really expecting it to show up.

Without being able to contain her excitement, Caroline bursts through the door when my mouth is still full of toothpaste.

She's jumping up and down, holding a box in her hand.

"Wait, what's that?" I mumble and wash my mouth out with water.

"This is it!" Caroline screeches and pulls me into the living room before I have a chance to wipe my mouth with a towel.

"But it's a box," I say staring at her.

"Okay, okay," Caroline takes a couple of deep yoga breaths, exhaling loudly.

She puts the box carefully on our dining room table. There's no address on it.

It looks something like a fancy gift box with a big monogrammed C in the middle.

Is the C for Caroline?

"Is this how it came? There's no address on it?" I ask.

"It was hand-delivered," Caroline whispers.

I hold my breath as she carefully removes the top part, revealing the satin and silk covered wood box inside.

The top of it is gold plated with whimsical twirls all around the edges, and the mirrored area is engraved with her full name.

Caroline Elizabeth Kennedy Spruce.

Underneath her name is a date, one week in the future. 8 PM.

We stare at it for a few moments until Caroline reaches for the elegant knob to open the box.

Inside, Caroline finds a custom monogram made of foil in gold on silk emblazoned on the inside of the flap cover.

There's also a folio covered in silk. Caroline carefully opens the folio and finds another foil monogram and the invitation.

The inside invitation is one layer, shimmer white, with gold writing.

"Is this for real? How many layers of invitation are there?" I ask.

But the presentation is definitely doing its job. We are both duly impressed.

"There's another knob," I say, pointing to the knob in front of the box.

I'm not sure how we had missed it before.

Caroline carefully pulls on this knob, revealing a drawer that holds the inserts (a card with directions and a response card).

"Oh my God, I can't go to this alone," Caroline mumbles, turning to me.

I stare blankly at her.

Getting invited to this party has been her dream ever since she found out about it from someone in the Cicada 17, a super-secret society at Yale.

"Look, here, it says that I can bring a friend," she yells out even though I'm standing right next to her.

"It probably says a date. A plus one?" I say.

"No, a friend. Girl preferred," Caroline reads off the invitation card.

That part of the invitation is in very small ink, as if someone made the person stick it on, without their express permission.

"I don't want to crash," I say.

Frankly, I don't really want to go.

These kind of upper-class events always make me feel a little bit uncomfortable.

"Hey, aren't you supposed to be at work?" I ask.

"Eh, I took a day off," Caroline says waving her arm. "I knew that the invitation would come today and I just couldn't deal with work. You know how it is."

I nod. Sort of.

Caroline and I seem like we come from the same world.

We both graduated from private school, we both went to Yale, and our parents belong to the same exclusive country club in Greenwich, Connecticut.

But we're not really that alike.

Caroline's family has had money for many generations going back to the railroads.

My parents were an average middle class family from Connecticut.

They were both teachers and our idea of summering was renting a 1-bedroom bungalow near Clearwater, FL for a week.

But then my parents got divorced when I was 8, and my mother started tutoring kids to make extra money.

The pay was the best in Greenwich, where parents paid more than $100 an hour.

And that's how she met, Mitch Willoughby, my stepfather.

He was a widower with a five-year old daughter who was not doing well after her mom's untimely death.

Even though Mom didn't usually tutor anyone younger than 12, she agreed to take a meeting with Mitch and his daughter because $200 an hour was too much to turn down.

Three months later, they were in love and six

months later, he asked her to marry him on top of the Eiffel Tower.

They got married, when I was 11, in a huge 450-person ceremony in Nantucket.

So even though Caroline and I run in the same circles, we're not really from the same circle.

It has nothing to do with her, she's totally accepting, it's me.

I don't always feel like I belong.

Caroline majored in art-history at Yale, and she now works at an exclusive contemporary art gallery in Soho.

It's chic and tiny, featuring only 3 pieces of art at a time.

Ash, the owner - I'm not sure if that's her first or last name - mainly keeps the space as a showcase. What the gallery really specializes in is going to wealthy people's homes and choosing their art for them.

They're basically interior designers, but only for art.

None of the pieces sell for anything less than $200 grand, but Caroline's take home salary is about $21,000.

Clearly, not enough to pay for our 2 bedroom apartment in Chelsea.

Her parents cover her part of the rent and pay all of her other expenses.

Mine do too, of course.

Well, Mitch does.

I only make about $27,000 at my writer's assistant job and that's obviously not covering my half of our $6,000 per month apartment.

So, what's the difference between me and Caroline?

I guess the only difference is that I feel bad about taking the money.

I have a $150,000 school loan from Yale that I don't want Mitch to pay for.

It's my loan and I'm going to pay for it myself, dammit.

Plus, unlike Caroline, I know that real people don't really live like this.

Real people like my dad, who is being pressured to sell the house for more than a million dollars that he and my mom bought back in the late 80's (the neighborhood has gone up in price and teachers now have to make way for tech entrepreneurs and real estate moguls).

"How can you just not go to work like that? Didn't you use all of your sick days flying to Costa Rica last month?" I ask.

"Eh, who cares? Ash totally understands. Besides, she totally owes me. If it weren't for me, she would've never closed that geek millionaire who had the hots for me and ended up buying close to a million dollars' worth of art for his new mansion."

Caroline does have a way with men.

She's fun and outgoing and perky.

The trick, she once told me, is to figure out exactly what the guy wants to hear.

Because a geek millionaire, as she calls anyone who has made money in tech, does not want to hear the same thing that a football player wants to hear.

And neither of them want to hear what a trust fund playboy wants to hear.

But Caroline isn't a gold digger.

Not at all.

Her family owns half the East Coast.

And when it comes to men, she just likes to have fun.

I look at the time.

It's my day off, but that doesn't mean that I want to spend it in bed in my pajamas, listening to Caroline obsessing over what she's going to wear.

No, today, is my day to actually get some writing done.

I'm going to Starbucks, getting a table in the

back, near the bathroom, and am actually going to finish this short story that I've been working on for a month.

Or maybe start a new one.

I go to my room and start getting dressed.

I have to wear something comfortable, but something that's not exactly work clothes.

I hate how all of my clothes have suddenly become work clothes. It's like they've been tainted.

They remind me of work and I can't wear them out anymore on any other occasion. I'm not a big fan of my work, if you can't tell.

Caroline follows me into my room and plops down on my bed.

I take off my pajamas and pull on a pair of leggings.

Ever since these have become the trend, I find myself struggling to force myself into a pair of jeans.

They're just so comfortable!

"Okay, I've come to a decision," Caroline says. "You *have* to come with me!"

"Oh, I have to come with you?" I ask, incredulously. "Yeah, no, I don't think so."

"Oh c'mon! Please! Pretty please! It will be so much fun!"

"Actually, you can't make any of those promises.

You have no idea what it will be," I say, putting on a long sleeve shirt and a sweater with a zipper in the front.

Layers are important during this time of year.

The leaves are changing colors, winds are picking up, and you never know if it's going to be one of those gorgeous warm, crisp New York days they like to feature in all those romantic comedies or a soggy, overcast dreary day that only shows up in one scene at the end when the two main characters fight or break up (but before they get back together again).

"Okay, yes, I see your point," Caroline says, sitting up and crossing her legs. "But here is what we *do* know. We do know that it's going to be amazing. I mean, look at the invitation. It's a freakin' box with engravings and everything!"

Usually, Caroline is much more eloquent and better at expressing herself.

"Okay, yes, the invitation is impressive," I admit.

"And as you know, the invitation is everything. I mean, it really sets the mood for the party. The event! And not just the mood. It establishes a certain expectation. And this box..."

"Yes, the invitation definitely sets up a certain expectation," I agree.

"So?"

"So?" I ask her back.

"Don't you want to find out what that expectation is?"

"No." I shake my head categorically.

"Okay. So what else do we know?" Caroline asks rhetorically as I pack away my Mac into my bag.

"I have to go, Caroline," I say.

"No, listen. The yacht. Of course, the yacht. How could I bury the lead like that?" She jumps up and down with excitement again.

"We also know that it's going to be this super exclusive event on a *yacht*! And not just some small 100 footer, but a *mega*-yacht."

I stare at her blankly, pretending to not be impressed.

When Caroline first found out about this party, through her ex-boyfriend, we spent days trying to figure out what made this event so special.

But given that neither of us have been on a yacht before, at least not a mega-yacht – we couldn't quite get it.

"You know the yacht is going to be amazing!"

"Yes, of course," I give in. "But that's why I'm sure that you're going to have a wonderful time by yourself. I have to go."

I grab my keys and toss them into the bag.

"Ellie," Caroline says.

The tone of her voice suddenly gets very serious, to match the grave expression on her face.

"Ellie, please. I don't think I can go by myself."

CHAPTER 2 - ELLIE

WHEN YOU HAVE COFFEE WITH A GUY YOU CAN'T HAVE...

*A*nd that's pretty much how I was roped into going.

You don't know Caroline, but if you did, the first thing you'd find out is that she is not one to take things seriously.

Nothing fazes her.

Nothing worries her.

Sometimes she is the most enlightened person on earth, other times she's the densest.

Most of the time, I'm jealous of the fact that she simply lives life in the present.

"So, you're going?" my friend Tom asks.

He brought me my pumpkin spice latte, the first one of the season!

I close my eyes and inhale it's sweet aroma before taking the first sip.

But even before its wonderful taste of cinnamon and nutmeg runs down my throat, Tom is already criticizing my decision.

"I can't believe you're actually going," he says.

"Oh my God, now I know it's officially fall," I change the subject.

"Was there actually such a thing as autumn before the pumpkin spice latte? I mean, I remember that we had falling leaves, changing colors, all that jazz, but without this...it's like Christmas without a Christmas tree."

"Ellie, it's a day after Labor Day," Tom rolls his eyes. "It's not fall yet."

I take another sip. "Oh yes, I do believe it is."

"Stop changing the subject," Tom takes a sip of his plain black coffee.

How he doesn't get bored with that thing, I'll never know.

But that's the thing about Tom.

He's reliable.

Always on time, never late.

It's nice. That's what I have always liked about him.

He's basically the opposite of Caroline in every way.

And that's what makes seeing him like this, as only a friend, so hard.

"Why are you going there? Can't Caroline go by herself?" Tom asks, looking straight into my eyes.

His hair has this annoying tendency of falling into his face just as he's making a point – as a way of accentuating it.

It's actually quite vexing especially given how irresistible it makes him look.

His eyes twinkle under the low light in the back of the Starbucks.

"I'm going as her plus one," I announce.

I make my voice extra perky on purpose.

So that it portrays excitement, rather than apprehensiveness, which is actually how I'm feeling over the whole thing.

"She's making you go as her plus one," Tom announces as a matter a fact. He knows me too well.

"I just don't get it, Ellie. I mean, why bother? It's a super yacht filled with filthy rich people. I mean, how fun can that party be?"

"Jealous much?" I ask.

"I'm not jealous at all!" He jumps back in his seat. "If that's what you think…"

He lets his words trail off and suddenly the conversation takes on a more serious mood.

"You don't have to worry, I'm not going to miss your engagement party," I say quietly. It's the weekend after I get back."

He shakes his head and insists that that's not what he's worried about.

"I just don't get it Ellie," he says.

You don't get it?

You don't get why I'm going?

I've had feelings for you for, what, two years now?

But the time was never right.

At first, I was with my boyfriend and the night of our breakup, you decided to kiss me.

You totally caught me off guard.

And after that long painful breakup, I wasn't ready for a relationship.

And you, my best friend, you weren't really a rebound contender.

And then, just as I was about to tell you how I felt, you spend the night with Carrie.

Beautiful, wealthy, witty Carrie. Carrie Warrenhouse, the current editor of BuzzPost, the online magazine where we both work, and the daughter of Edward Warrenhouse, the owner of BuzzPost.

Oh yeah, and on top of all that, you also started seeing her and then asked her to marry you.

And now you two are getting married on Valentine's Day.

And I'm really happy for you.

Really.

Truly.

The only problem is that I'm also in love with you.

And now, I don't know what the hell to do with all of this except get away from New York.

Even if it's just for a few days.

But of course, I can't say any of these things.

Especially the last part.

"This hasn't been the best summer," I say after a few moments. "And I just want to do something fun. Get out of town. Go to a party. Because that's all this is, a party."

"That's not what I heard," Tom says.

"What do you mean?"

"Ever since you told me you were going, I started looking into this event.

And the rumor is that it's not what it is."

I shake my head, roll my eyes.

"What? You don't believe me?" Tom asks incredulously.

I shake my head.

"Okay, what? What did you hear?"

"It's basically like a Playboy Mansion party on steroids. It's totally out of control. Like one big orgy."

"And you would know what a Playboy Mansion party is like," I joke.

"I'm being serious, Ellie. I'm not sure this is a good place for you. I mean, you're not Caroline."

"And what the hell does that mean?" I ask.

Now, I'm actually insulted.

At first, I was just listening because I thought he was being protective.

But now...

"What you don't think I'm fun enough? You don't think I like to have a good time?" I ask.

"That's not what I meant," Tom backtracks. I start to gather my stuff. "What are you doing?"

"No, you know what," I stop packing up my stuff. "I'm not leaving. You're leaving."

"Why?"

"Because I came here to write. I have work to do. I staked out this table and I'm not leaving until I have something written. I thought you wanted to have coffee with me. I thought we were friends. I didn't realize that you came here to chastise me about my decisions."

"That's not what I'm doing," Tom says, without getting out of his chair.

"You have to leave Tom. I want you to leave."

"I just don't understand what happened to us," he says getting up, reluctantly.

I stare at him as if he has lost his mind.

"You have no right to tell me what I can or can't do. You don't even have the right to tell your fiancée. Unless you don't want her to stay your fiancée for long."

"I'm not trying to tell you what to do, Ellie. I'm just worried. This super exclusive party on some mega-yacht, that's not you. That's not us."

"Not us? You've got to be kidding," I shake my head. "You graduated from Princeton, Tom. Your father is an attorney at one of the most prestigious law-firms in Boston. He has argued cases before the Supreme Court. You're going to marry the heir to the Warrenhouse fortune. I'm so sick and tired of your working class hero attitude, I can't even tell you. Now, are you going to leave or should I?"

The disappointment that I saw in Tom's eyes hurt me to my very soul.

But he had hurt me.

His engagement came completely out of left field.

I had asked him to give me some time after my breakup and after waiting for only two months, he started dating Carrie.

And then they moved in together. And then he asked her to marry him.

And throughout all that, he just sort of pretended that we were still friends.

Just like none of this ever happened.

I open my computer and stare at the half written story before me.

Earlier today, before Caroline, before Tom, I had all of these ideas.

I just couldn't wait to get started.

But now...I doubted that I could even spell my name right.

Staring at a non-moving blinker never fuels the writing juices.

I close my computer and look around the place.

All around me, people are laughing and talking.

Leggings and Uggs are back in season – even though the days are still warm and crispy.

It hasn't rained in close to a week and everyone's

good mood seems to be energized by the bright rays of the afternoon sun.

Last spring, I was certain that Tom and I would get together over the summer and I would spend the fall falling in love with my best friend.

And now?

Now, he's engaged to someone else.

Not just someone else – my boss!

And we just had a fight over some stupid party that I don't even really want to go to.

He's right, of course.

It's not my style.

My family might have money, but that's not the world in which I'm comfortable.

I'm always standing on the sidelines and it's not going to be any different at this party.

But if I don't go now, after this, that means that I'm listening to him.

And he has no right to tell me what to do.

So, I have to go.

How did everything get so messed up?

CHAPTER 3 - ELLIE

"What the hell are you still doing hanging out with that asshole?" Caroline asks dismissively.

We are in Elle's, a small boutique in Soho, where you can shop by appointment only.

I didn't even know these places existed until Caroline introduced me to the concept.

Caroline is not a fan of Tom.

They never got along, not since he called her an East Side snob at our junior year Christmas party at Yale and she called him a middle class poseur.

Neither insult was very creative, but their insults got better over the years as their hatred for each other grew.

You know how in the movies, two characters who

hate each other in the beginning always end up falling in love by the end?

Well, for a while, I actually thought that would happen to them.

If not fall in love, at least hook up. But no, they stayed steadfast in their hatred.

"That guy is such a tool. I mean, who the hell is he to tell you what to do anyway? It's not like you're his girlfriend," Caroline says placing a silver beaded bandage dress to her body and extending her right leg in front.

Caroline is definitely a knock out.

She's 5'10", 125 pounds with legs that go up to her chin.

In fact, from far away, she seems to be all blonde hair and legs and nothing else.

"I think he was just concerned, given all the stuff that is out there about this party."

"Okay, first of all, you have to stop calling it a party."

"Why? What is it?"

"It's not a party. It's like calling a wedding a party. Is it a party? Yes. But is it bigger than that."

"I had no idea that you were so sensitive to language. Fine. What do you want me to call it?'

"An experience," she announces, completely seriously.

"Are you kidding me? No way. There's no way I'm going to call it an experience."

We browse in silence for a few moments.

Some of the dresses and tops and shoes are pretty, some aren't.

I'm the first to admit that I do not have the vocabulary or knowledge to appreciate a place like this.

Now, Caroline on the other hand…

"Oh my God, I'm just in love with all these one of a kind pieces you have here," she says to the woman upfront who immediately starts to beam with pride.

"That's what we're going for."

"These statement bags and the detailing on these booties – agh! To die for, right?" Caroline says and they both turn to me.

"Yeah, totally," I agree blindly.

"And these high-end core pieces, I could just wear this every day!" Caroline pulls up a rather structured cream colored short sleeve shirt with a tassel hem and a boxy fit.

I'm not sure what makes that shirt a so-called core piece, but I go with the flow.

I'm out of my element and I know it.

"Okay, so what are we supposed to wear to this *experience* if we don't even know what's going to be going on there."

"I'm not exactly sure but definitely not jeans and t-shirts," Caroline says referring to my staple outfit. "But the invitation also said not to worry. They have all the necessities if we forget something."

As I continue to aimlessly browse, my mind starts to wander.

And goes back to Tom.

I met Tom at the Harvard-Yale game.

He was my roommate's boyfriend's high school best friend and he came up for the weekend to visit him.

We became friends immediately.

One smile from him, even on Skype, made all of my worries disappear.

He just sort of got me, the way no one really did.

After graduation, we applied to work a million different online magazines and news outlets, but BuzzPost was the one place that took both of us.

We didn't exactly plan to end up at the same place, but it was a nice coincidence.

He even asked if I wanted to be his roommate – but I had already agreed to room with Caroline.

He ended up in this crappy fourth floor walkup

in Hell's Kitchen – one of the only buildings that they haven't gentrified yet.

So, the rent was still somewhat affordable. Like I said, Tom likes to think of himself as a working class hero even though his upbringing is far from it.

Whenever he came over to our place, he always made fun of how expensive the place was, but it was always in good fun.

At least, it felt like it at the time.

Now?

I'm not so sure anymore.

"Do you think that Tom is really going to get married?" I ask Caroline while we're changing.

She swings my curtain open in front of the whole store.

I'm topless, but luckily I'm facing away from her and the assistant is buried in her phone.

"What are you doing?" I shriek and pull the curtain closed.

"What are you thinking?" she demands.

I manage to grab a shirt and cover myself before Caroline pulls the curtain open again.

She is standing before me in only a bra and a matching pair of panties – completely confident and unapologetic.

I think she's my spirit animal.

"Who cares about Tom?" Caroline demands.

"I do," I say meekly.

"Well, you shouldn't. He's a dick. You are way too good for him. I don't even understand what you see in him."

"He's my friend," I say as if that explains everything.

Caroline knows how long I've been in love with Tom.

She knows everything.

At times, I wish I hadn't been so open.

But other times, it's nice to have someone to talk to.

Even if she isn't exactly understanding.

"You can't just go around pining for him, Ellie. You can do so much better than him. You were with your ex and he just hung around waiting and waiting. Never telling you how he felt. Never making any grand gestures."

Caroline is big on gestures.

The grander the better.

She watches a lot of movies and she demands them of her dates.

And the funny thing is that you often get exactly what you ask from the world.

"I don't care about that," I say. "We were in the wrong place for each other.

I was with someone and then I wasn't ready to jump into another relationship right away.

And then...he and Carrie got together."

"There's no such thing as not the right time. Life is what you make it, Ellie. You're in control of your life. And I hate the fact that you're acting like you're not the main character in your own movie."

"I don't even know what you're talking about," I say.

"All I'm saying is that you deserve someone who tells you how he feels. Someone who isn't afraid of rejection. Someone who isn't afraid to put it all out there."

"Maybe that's who you want," I say.

"And that's not who you want?" Caroline says taking a step back away from me.

I think about it for a moment.

"Well, no I wouldn't say that. It is who I want," I finally say. "But I had a boyfriend then. And Tom and I were friends. So I couldn't expect him to—"

"You couldn't expect him to put it all out there? Tell you how he feels and take the risk of getting hurt?" Caroline cuts me off.

I hate to admit it, but that's exactly what I want.

That's exactly what I wanted from him back then.

I didn't want him to just hang around being my friend, making me question my feelings for him.

And if he had done that, if he had told me how he felt about me earlier, before my awful breakup, then I would've jumped in.

I would've broken up with my ex immediately to be with him.

"So, is that what I should do now? Now that things are sort of reversed?" I ask.

"What do you mean?"

"I mean, now that he's the one in the relationship. Should I just put it all out there? Tell him how I feel. Leave it all on the table, so to speak."

Caroline takes a moment to think about this.

I appreciate it because I know how little she thinks of him.

"Because I don't know if I can," I add quietly.

"Maybe that's your answer right there," Caroline finally says. "If you did want him, really want him to be yours, then you wouldn't be able to not to. You'd have to tell him."

I go back into my dressing room and pull the curtain closed.

I look at myself in the mirror.

The pale girl with green eyes and long dark hair is a coward.

She is afraid of life.

Afraid to really live.

Would this ever change?

CHAPTER 4 - ELLIE

WHEN YOU DECIDE TO LIVE YOUR LIFE...

"*A*re you ready?" Caroline bursts into my room. "Our cab is downstairs."

No, I'm not ready.

Not at all.

But I'm going.

I take one last look in the mirror and grab my suitcase.

As the cab driver loads our bags into the trunk, Caroline takes my hand, giddy with excitement.

Excited is not how I would describe my state of being.

More like reluctant.

And terrified.

When I get into the cab, my stomach drops and I feel like I'm going to throw up.

But then the feeling passes.

"I can't believe this is actually happening," I say.

"I know, right? I'm so happy you're doing this with me, Ellie. I mean, really. I don't know if I could go by myself."

After ten minutes of meandering through the convoluted streets of lower Manhattan, the cab drops us off in front of a nondescript office building.

"Is the party here?" I ask.

Caroline shakes her head with a little smile on her face.

She knows something I don't know.

I can tell by that mischievous look on her face.

"What's going on?" I ask.

But she doesn't give in.

Instead, she just nudges me inside toward the security guard at the front desk.

She hands him a card, he nods, and shows us to the elevator.

"Top floor," he says.

When we reach the top floor, the elevator doors swing open on the roof and a strong gust of wind knocks into me.

Out of the corner of my eye, I see it.

The helicopter.

The blades are already going.

A man approaches us and takes our bags.

"What are we doing here?" I yell on top of my lungs.

But Caroline doesn't hear me.

I follow her inside the helicopter, ducking my head to make sure that I get in all in one piece.

A few minutes later, we take off.

We fly high above Manhattan, maneuvering past the buildings as if we're birds.

I've never been in a helicopter before and, a part of me, wishes that I'd had some time to process this beforehand.

"I didn't tell you because I thought you would freak," Caroline says into her headset.

She knows me too well.

She pulls out her phone and we pose for a few selfies.

"It's beautiful up here," I say looking out the window.

In the afternoon sun, the Manhattan skyline is breathtaking.

The yellowish red glow bounces off the glass buildings and shimmers in the twilight.

I don't know where we are going, but for the first time in a long time, I don't care.

I stay in the moment and enjoy it for everything it's worth.

Quickly the skyscrapers and the endless parade of bridges disappear and all that remains below us is the glistening of the deep blue sea.

And then suddenly, somewhere in the distance I see it.

The yacht.

At first, it appears as barely a speck on the horizon.

But as we fly closer, it grows in size.

By the time we land, it seems to be the size of its own island.

———

A TALL, beautiful woman waves to us as we get off the helicopter.

She's holding a plate with glasses of champagne and nods to a man in a tuxedo next to her to take our bags.

"Wow, that was quite an entrance," Caroline says to me.

"Mr. Black knows how to welcome his guests," the woman says. "My name is Lizbeth and I am here to serve you."

Lizbeth shows us around the yacht and to our stateroom.

"There will be cocktails right outside when you're ready," Lizbeth said before leaving us alone.

As soon as she left, we grabbed hands and let out a big yelp.

"Oh my God! Can you believe this place?" Caroline asks.

"No, it's amazing," I say, running over to the balcony. The blueness of the ocean stretched out as far as the eye could see.

"Are you going to change for cocktails?" Caroline asks, sitting down at the vanity. "The helicopter did a number on my hair."

We both crack up laughing.

Neither of us have ever been on a helicopter before – let alone a boat this big.

I decide against a change of clothes – my Nordstrom leggings and polka dot blouse should do just fine for cocktail hour.

But I do slip off my pair of flats and put on a nice pair of pumps, to dress up the outfit a little bit.

While Caroline changes into her short black dress, I brush the tangles out of my hair and reapply my lipstick.

"Ready?" Caroline asks.

CHAPTER 5 - ELLIE

*M*uch to our surprise, when we get to the living room at the end of the hallway, there's no one there.

Not a single soul. I make my way through the French doors and onto the deck outside, but there's no one there either.

"Are we just supposed to wait here?" Caroline asks. I shrug.

After a few minutes, Lizbeth reappears with one garment bag swung over her shoulder.

"Are we in the wrong place?" I ask.

"I'm terribly sorry. But Mr. Black wants you to wear this."

I stare at her for a moment.

Before it hits me that she's talking to me.

"What?"

Lizbeth repeats the statement verbatim, without offering a single additional word of explanation.

"What's wrong with what I'm wearing?" I ask.

A flash of heat pounces through my body.

I turn to Caroline for some backup. But instead of offering her support, she grabs my arm and takes me back to our stateroom.

"What's going on?" I ask. "What's wrong with what I'm wearing?" I demand.

She looks me up and down and shakes her head.

"I don't know. That's actually a very nice outfit."

I know she's telling the truth because Caroline would never lie about something as important as fashion.

She opens the garment bag.

A part of me is still expecting it to contain two outfits.

But no, it just has one.

A short, sheer, red dress.

Strapless.

"I'm not wearing this."

There's a loud knock on the door.

"Is everything alright in there?" Lizbeth asks through the door.

"I'm not wearing this!" I say loud enough for her to hear.

"Yes, she is," Caroline says. "We're fine. We'll be out in a few minutes."

I stare at Caroline with a perplexed look on my face.

"This is a beautiful dress. Numi. Her stuff is basically impossible to get. Really high end."

I cross my arms. "I don't care," I say.

Caroline takes the dress and presses it to her body.

She looks into the mirror with a forlorn look on her face.

"Seriously, Ellie. This dress is major!"

"I don't care. Who the hell is he to tell me what to wear? I mean what kind of manners is that? And who the hell is Mr. Black anyway?"

"I don't know. And that's what I can't wait to find out. And for us to find out, you have to put on this dress."

I shake my head no.

She continues to pester me.

Minutes tick away and neither of us give in.

"If you insist on being such a baby, I'm going to go out there by myself," Caroline finally says.

"Seriously? Who the hell does he think he is telling me what to wear?"

We go back and forth for a few more minutes.

Eventually, I let up.

I don't want to stay in this room all by myself all evening.

And clearly, I can't go out without putting this on.

I go into the bathroom for some privacy.

Caroline has seen me naked on occasion but something about this dress is extra uncomfortable.

It's not like I'm putting on my own clothes.

I pull off my leggings and blouse.

I hold the dress out in front of me and realize that I'm going to have to remove my bra as well.

Damn.

Slipping the dress over my head, I pray that it fits.

My prayers are answered.

It does!

After zipping it on the side, I look in the mirror.

It's short, but incredibly flattering.

It hugs me in all the right places, accentuating only my best features.

"You're gorgeous!" Caroline's jaw drops open when I come out of the bathroom.

I nod. I hate to admit it, but it is quite pretty.

"I can't believe they didn't give me something like this to wear," Caroline says as we walk back out into the living room. "That's it, next time I'm showing up in a brown paper bag so they'll have no choice."

CHAPTER 6 - ELLIE

WHEN YOU MEET A BROODING STRANGER...

*T*his time the living room is filled with people.

Really attractive people.

Men in their twenties and early thirties are crowding around the bar.

Others are sitting in leather chairs and on the couch.

Beautiful women walk around with cocktails in their hands as if they own the place.

Many are already coupled up – sitting close to each other with their legs pointing toward their partners.

Caroline heads straight to the bar and orders us two martinis. I'm happy to have a drink to relax me. Liquid courage, so to speak.

Out of the corner of my eye, I spot one man sitting all by himself.

He's one of the most attractive guys here.

But it's the serious, brooding look on his face that really makes him stand out.

I wonder if maybe one of his friends dragged him here as well.

I take two big sips of my martini.

Following Caroline's lead, I take a seat at one of the bar stools.

She has a way of positioning herself in such a way that she's half facing the room.

This way, she can talk to me and still let any interested parties out there know that it's okay to approach.

Two guys quickly take the bait.

No cheesy pickup lines here. Just straight out introductions. Ben is the taller one with honey blonde hair and grey eyes. He's the one who seems more interested in me. Alex's deep blue eyes are glued to Caroline.

Within a few minutes, we find out that they are both finance bros – investment bankers who work on Wall Street.

Ben went to Brown and Alex to Dartmouth.

They found out about the party pretty much the same way that Caroline did.

Someone in a secret society talked who shouldn't have.

I don't know whether the person was from the Cicada 17 or not.

"At first, we didn't know if this was a girl-only party," Alex says. "But as we found out more and more about it, we realized that it was just an awesome party."

"Our boss, Logan, has been to one of these events, but no matter how much we pushed, he would not tell us a thing about it," Ben boasted. "Except that there's a masquerade ball."

"Masquerade ball?" I ask.

"Yes, apparently only some of us from today will be invited to stay for the main attraction. But, honestly, I heard so many rumors about this place, who the hell knows which ones are true, right?" Ben says and we all laugh.

Caroline laughs the loudest, tossing her hair from one side to the other.

Neither Ben nor Alex can seem to pull their eyes off her.

And then, the hair on the back of my neck stands up.

I'm facing the bar, away from the rest of the room.

But I can't help but feel someone look at me. From behind.

Slowly, I turn on the barstool and look around.

His dark piercing eyes stare at me from across the room.

He's dressed in an elegant expensive suit.

It's exquisitely tailored for his long lean body.

His hair is thick, the color of dark chocolate.

The man sits back in his plush chair at the far end of the room.

He's the only one not mingling or laughing. Not even smiling.

His eyes meet mine and don't let go.

After a few moments, I get so uncomfortable, I can't bear to hold his gaze anymore.

And yet, he maintains his with grace and ease.

"Who's that?" I ask, turning away from him. "Don't look now," I add, but it's too late.

Ben, Alex, and Caroline all look over at the stranger at the same time.

My cheeks flush in embarrassment.

"I don' know," they all shrug and say almost simultaneously.

The three of them don't seem to be very

concerned with the serious look on the stranger's face and quickly go back to chatting among themselves.

But I can't look away.

There's something that's pulling me toward him.

His eyes – are brilliant and deep – the color of the ocean – and they mesmerize me.

I look over again, watch him watching me, and then look away.

His gaze is disarming, it makes me feel naked and exposed, and I cannot hold it for long.

And yet, I yearn to look at him again.

"If you're so interested in that guy, why don't you just go over and talk to him," Caroline says, finishing her drink.

The thought of that sends shivers down my body.

"I can't just go over there…And say what?"

"Tell him your name and ask him how he got here," she says with a casual shrug. "This isn't like in a bar. You have the perfect pickup line all ready and set to go."

"No, I can't," I shake my head and order another martini. More liquid courage is in order.

"Hi there," a deep voice startles me.

Before I have the chance to turn around, I see a big wide smile sweep over Caroline's face.

"Well, hello there, stranger. I'm Caroline," she says extending her hand. "This is Ben, Alex, and Ellie."

How can she do that?

Be so casual and confident.

Does nothing faze her?

I take a deep breath and look up.

It's him.

The guy from the plush chair.

The lonely stranger.

I know that it's him before even turning around.

When I finally do turn, my gaze lands on his broad shoulders and the thick weave of his pristine suit.

My eyes slowly pan up to his face.

Strong square jaw.

Confident nose.

Tan skin.

Hair so thick and gorgeous that it's begging to be stroked.

And those eyes....ahhh!

"I'm Blake Garrison," he says quietly.

My heart skips a beat.

The top of his lips curl up into half a smile.

They are lush and shiny.

When he licks his lips, my heart skips another beat.

"So, what brings you to the party Blake?" Ben asks.

"Same as you, I gather," Blake says and turns his eyes toward me.

"I was wondering if I could have a word with you," he says. "In private."

Caroline's eyes get wide.

Aren't we a little unacquainted for private words? I wonder.

"Um, sure," I shrug and follow him to the other end of the bar.

It's not exactly private, but we are outside of earshot from the rest of the guests.

"You shouldn't be here," Blake says.

Carefully.

Meticulously.

Each word comes out with great difficulty.

"What?"

"You shouldn't be here," he repeats himself.

This time, the words come out almost robotically.

"I don't understand. Why?"

My eyes search his face for an answer.

What could he possibly mean?

Suddenly, I notice that his eyes are inspecting my face just as feverishly.

"I didn't mean to scare you," he says quietly. "You just shouldn't be here."

"Why?" I ask.

And suddenly, my moment of fear morphs into anger.

Who the hell does he think he is telling me where I should and shouldn't be?

"Because you don't belong here," he says.

His eyes suddenly become overcome with sadness.

But I've had enough of his cryptic games.

"And you would know that, *how* exactly?" I ask.

The question is rhetorical.

I don't wait for an answer.

Instead, I walk away.

"Ellie!" he hisses.

But I don't turn around.

Instead, I walk over to Caroline and take her arm.

"Are you okay?" she asks.

I nod.

"Let's have another round of drinks," I announce. "They're on me."

"The drinks are free, miss," the bartender reminds me.

Another version of me would feel bad over the social faux pas, but I just let it go.

The martini that I did have is already having an effect and I feel braver and stronger than I had before.

Plus, walking away from that rude asshole was a statement.

A moment of empowerment.

"Are you okay?" Caroline asks again.

I can tell that she's sensing that something's wrong.

"What did he say to you?"

"He's a weirdo," I announce. "He said that I shouldn't be here."

Caroline shakes her head.

"Yeah, he just came out and said that out loud.

I mean, is it just me, or is that a really rude thing to say?" I add. Caroline shrugs.

CHAPTER 7 - ELLIE

WHEN ANOTHER STRANGER INTRIGUES YOU...

*T*he rest of the cocktail hour proceeds without incident.

Thanks to Caroline, we meet almost everyone in the room and get the basic info about them.

95% of them are Ivy League grads and the other 5% went to prestigious liberal arts schools like Swarthmore and Wellesley.

Many work in finance and tech, some head non-profits and the rest are entrepreneurs.

They all heard about the party one way or another through friends of friends and no one really knows what to expect.

And none of them know the identity of the mysterious Mr. Black.

After mingling for what seems like forever, I

decide to get some fresh air and get away from the stuffiness of all those pleasantries.

Caroline is totally in her element – smiling, nodding, laughing at just the right times.

Putting everyone at ease.

Becoming everyone's best friend.

But I find that kind of stuff exhausting.

Even after a half an hour of it, I'm ready to tear my hair out.

"I'm sorry, but I have to go to the ladies room," I extricate myself from the tall, redheaded guy from Princeton who is on his second story about squash (the game, not the vegetable).

I didn't know it was possible for one person to have more than one story about squash, but apparently it is.

"Okay, hurry back," he says flashing me a smile.

Though his self-confidence and sense of his own importance are quite staggering, he is quite mesmerizing.

For a second, I get lost in his eyes and almost forget to walk away.

"Ellie? You okay?" he takes my arm, bringing me back to reality.

"Oh right, sorry," I mumble. "I'll be right back."

What was his name again?

Dax?

Wyatt?

Delacorte?

I've never been great with names, and my memory for matching faces with names is particularly bad at this party.

They're all so good looking and their names just seem to all blur together.

As I make my way away from him, I feel the Princeton guy's eyes on me burning into the back of my head.

So, instead of walking straight onto the deck from the main room, I head toward the hallway with the bathroom and then outside.

When I finally get outside, I inhale a deep breath of fresh salty air.

That one breath is quickly followed up by another and another.

Suddenly, all the boredom that had infected me during the cocktail hour vanishes and the chill of the outside air infuses me with new found energy.

"Well, hello there," a deep voice says.

It belongs to a man and it's coming from somewhere behind me.

Great, another boring conversation coming up.

I roll my eyes before turning to face him.

"Sometimes you just have to get out of there, right?" the man says.

That piques my interest. Intrigued, I turn around.

"Are you not having a good time?" I ask.

"Eh," the man shrugs casually, looking far into the blueness.

The sun is hovering just over the horizon, dipping in and out of the sea, as if it isn't sure if it wants to take the plunge.

"Isn't the sunset beautiful?" the man asks without taking his eyes off it.

I turn to face him.

He's dressed in an impeccable black suit.

His starched collar is unbuttoned and the sleeves of his suit are rolled up.

He isn't wearing a tie.

It suddenly hits me.

He must be the only guy here without a tie!

"Yes," I agree unable to pull my gaze away from him.

Casually, the man leans over the railing, staring into the distance.

The wind casually tosses around his short, honey blonde hair without bothering him one bit.

"So, where did you go to school?" I ask.

This has been the go-to conversation starter throughout the cocktail party and bad habits die hard.

I'm not really interested, but frankly I can't think of anything else to ask.

"Oh c'mon," he says turning to face me. "We can do better than that."

Before I have the chance to figure out how to respond, the man effortlessly pulls himself up to the railing and sits on top of it.

"Oh my God, what are you doing?" I gasp. "You're going to fall off."

The railing is made of thick wood, reinforced by thin pieces of metal laid out in horizontal slats.

Just over it, are the whites of the waves that crash into the ship.

"No, I'm not," he says with a coy smile, wrapping his feet around one of the horizontal slats.

He puts his hand on mine. Suddenly, I realize that my hand is on his thigh and I quickly remove it.

"You can keep it there," he says. "It feels nice."

"You're going to fall," I say with exasperation.

He's toying with me. I can feel it.

Making me mad.

And he's doing it on purpose.

"So, you're not having a good time at the party?" he asks, brushing the windswept hair out of my face.

I take a step back as soon as I feel his warm hand on my face.

"I wouldn't say that," I say.

"So, is that what you are doing here, on the deck, all by your lonesome? Getting away from everyone?"

Is this guy for real?

Ever since my mom married Mitch, I've become quite acquainted with the kind of confidence that runs through the blood of those who summer in the Hamptons.

But this guy, he's taking it to a whole new level.

After a moment of silence, he jumps off the railing and positions himself right in front of me.

"I'm Harrison. Harrison Brooks. But people just call me Brooks."

"Hi," I say unamused.

I'm getting quite sick of how casually he infringes on my personal space– both vertical and horizontal.

"And you are?" he asks, taking a step closer.

I can feel his breath on my face. Even though I'm angry and annoyed, I find it intoxicating.

"Ellie," I say, reluctantly extending my hand.

"Do you have a last name Ellie?" he asks shaking my hand.

"Yes," I say and turn to walk away from him. Not that you're getting it.

"You have spunk, Ellie," Brooks yells after me. "I like that."

As I make my way around the empty deck, my mind wanders back to Brooks.

Maybe I should've stayed.

Perhaps I was a bit rude.

No, he was the one who was rude.

Sitting up on the railing.

Coming too close to me.

Breaking all rules of social conduct and politeness.

Who the hell does he think he is?

And yet despite all of these things – or perhaps because of them – I couldn't stop myself from thinking about him.

His deep blue eyes.

His soft lips.

His arrogant demeanor.

His shiny hair.

Agh, someone stop me!

I walk back into the main room where the cocktail party was still supposed to be in full bloom.

But much to my surprise, it isn't.

"Where is everyone?" I ask one of the servants who is wiping down the tables.

How long was I out there?

I wonder to myself.

"Back in their rooms, I guess," he says with a shrug.

CHAPTER 8 - ELLIE

WHEN YOU THINK THE PARTY IS OVER, BUT IT'S JUST
BEGINNING…

*W*hen I get back to our room, I find Caroline lying on top of her bed in her dress.

She has a concerned look on her face and she's picking at her newly polished nails.

"What's wrong?" I ask.

"This is it," she says. "Now, we're actually going to find out who is going to stay and who is going to go."

I don't know what she means exactly.

But she's quick to explain that apparently the cocktail party was a type of sorting event.

Not every person who attends gets to stay on for the main event.

"Do you mean the masquerade ball?" I ask.

"I don't really know," she shrugs. "There are so many rumors flying around."

I sit down in front of the vanity and examine my face.

I'm tempted to pull off my eyelashes, but Caroline stops me before I start.

"Don't you dare take off your makeup, or change. There's going to be more stuff going on tonight and you don't want to get dressed all over again."

I roll my eyes.

There's no way I'm doing anything more today.

All I want to do right now is take off these high heels, peel myself out of this tight dress and relax with a bag of chips in my sweats.

Being this fabulous is exhausting.

But then again, if there are more festivities on the way, I definitely don't want to go through the trouble of changing back into this damn thing.

"Okay, but I'm not waiting long," I say, glancing at the time. "One hour tops."

I flip on the television, and click through the channels.

Caroline fixes her lipstick and checks her teeth for any stains.

I grab a water out of the minibar and spill some of it on my dress when I open it.

"Shit," I say, patting the spot dry, without much luck.

Suddenly, there's a knock at the door.

Caroline freezes. I roll my eyes and open the door.

"Will you two please join me in the main cabin in five minutes?" Lizbeth asks.

I look her up and down.

She's dressed in a completely different outfit.

This time, she's wearing a long black dress, which cinches her tiny waist in a corset and pushes her perfect breasts up to the sky.

"Yes, sure," I say.

Lizbeth flashes a polite but disapproving smile.

As soon as I close the door, Caroline practically jumps on me.

"Oh my God! Oh my God!" she shrieks. "Do you know what this means?"

"No, not really."

"We made an impression. They want us."

"For what?"

I stump her for a moment with the question.

She stares at me as if I just asked her to multiply 345 by 257 in her head.

"I have no idea!" she screams, and runs over to

the vanity to check her hair and makeup and dress again.

"Do you think we both have to go?" I ask.

"What?" she turns around, nearly dropping the perfume bottle in her hand.

"Listen, the cocktail hour was fun, but I'm tired. I mean, this has been kind of a long day."

"Ellie, you HAVE to go! You just have to go."

I shake my head.

Given her level of excitement, there's no way that I'm going to get out of this anytime soon.

I decide to just suck it up and get on with it.

The sooner this starts, the sooner it will be over.

When we get to the main cabin, there are women everywhere.

And I do mean everywhere.

They are sitting on the couches, at the bar, at the tables.

They are all dressed impeccably in gorgeous dresses and high heels.

Some have short hair, but very few.

Most fall into the model category of physical beauty - impossibly tall, thin, and fabulous.

Some have large breasts, some small breasts.

"Where are all the men?" I ask Caroline.

"I have no idea, maybe they're in another room?"

After Caroline and I get our drinks at the bar, we position ourselves near the far wall.

All the seats are already taken.

Lizbeth clinks her glass to get our attention.

She's standing at the front of the yacht, surrounded entirely by windows.

Everyone looks up and quiets down when she clicks the glass a second time.

"Ladies. Thank you all for joining us today. It has really been a pleasure to serve you all."

There's that word again.

Serve.

Is it just me, or is that a really unusual word to use.

There are so many other ones like 'it has really been a pleasure to host you' or 'it has really been a pleasure to have you here.' But serve?

"So, let me take this time to fill you in about what's going to happen.

I know that there have been a lot of rumors flying around about what happens on this yacht party and I'm going to tell you."

"Oh my God, I'm so excited, I'm going to pee my pants!" Caroline hisses into my ear.

"Tonight, we have a very special attraction planned. We are going to have an auction."

A hush goes over the room.

Oh great, I think to myself.

I don't have any money.

Auctions are only fun for people who have free cash to spend.

"But it's not your typical auction. None of you will be expected to buy anything. In fact, it's more exciting than that."

Well, that's good, I think to myself.

At least, this isn't some elaborate charity ball auction where you're expected to spend at least a few grand to attend.

I've been to those plenty when Mitch's firm bought a table and expected the partners to fill it with their wives and children.

Those auctions were never as fun as the organizers seemed to think they were.

"Mr. Black's auction is nothing like any other auction you might have ever been to or may have heard of. What makes it particularly special is that, if you choose to participate, you will be the item that's auctioned off."

Wait, a second, I turn to Caroline.

Did I just hear that right?

"Let me explain. The men you have all met today at the cocktail hour are just some of the men who will be bidding in the auction. If you choose to participate, you will stand up on the stage and the men will bid on you. What they're bidding on is a night with you to do with whatever they want. Sexually speaking."

"What the hell?" I whisper to Caroline.

But she is completely mesmerized by Lizbeth, hanging on her every word.

"And in the morning, you will get a check for the winning bid."

A woman in front of me raises her hand. Lizbeth calls on her.

"So, how much exactly do women here go for?"

"Oh yes, of course," Lizbeth smiles. "Now, we don't know exactly how the bidding process will go, so we can't make promises. But you have all been pre-selected and you're all very beautiful. And the men in this room have a lot of money. It's not unusual for women to fetch 80 or $90,000. Some go for $150,000. We've even had one who went for $300,000."

Holy shit.

Did I just hear that correctly?

My school loans for four-years of college are $150,000. Would I really get a check for that much?

This seems just too good to be true.

"And what does it mean that the men get to do whatever they want? Sexually speaking?" the girl to the right of me asks.

"It means exactly that. Some men will want to talk and then have a little sex. Others want only oral. Others want everything. Oral. Them on top. You on top. Him in your ass. You in his ass with a strap on. Whatever floats his boat."

"And what if we haven't done anal before?" another girl asks.

"Well, I'm sure you can tell him that and he will be much more gentle. There will also, of course, be plenty of lubricants available."

"Are you going to do it?" Caroline whispers to me.

I shrug.

I hate to admit it, but there is something tempting about this.

The guys were really hot.

I wouldn't have minded sleeping with one or two of them on this yacht party for free.

"Okay, if there are no more questions, I will pass out the contracts. Please read it carefully. If you are willing to be auctioned off, please sign it and return it to me. The auction will begin in an hour. If you are not interested in the auction, you will take the helicopter back to the mainland. Unfortunately, you will not be joining us for the next part of the festivities."

She makes her way around the room, handing each of us a piece of paper and a pen.

I read over the contract carefully.

"This looks pretty standard," Caroline says. I look at her like she's insane.

"Pretty standard? There's nothing standard about this."

"Well, you know what I mean. It just lays out everything that she just told us. Plus, look at this part here. As soon as the auction is over, before the night actually commences, they will wire you the full amount to the account of your choice or give a check."

"You think they're good for it?" I joke.

"From the looks of this yacht, I'd say they are."

I've been around plenty of rich people, but the thought of someone actually writing a check or wiring eighty or ninety grand into my account seems unbelievable.

"I wonder why it has to be before the night commences," I say, reading the contract.

Lizbeth overhears me.

"Because everything that happens here is optional. It's up to you."

Now, that doesn't really make much sense, but I don't question her. After she leaves, I turn back to Caroline.

"I think it's because then it would be prostitution. Now, it's just some sort of present or a game or something," I say.

Caroline and I both sit there for a few minutes debating whether we should really go through with this.

Honestly, I don't know.

On one hand, it seems insane.

An auction.

A sex auction, in this day and age.

We're women.

We're supposed to be liberated and free.

We can have sex with anyone we choose.

On the other hand, being liberated and free also means that I'm free to participate in an auction if I want.

Right?

Would this really make me a prostitute?

Or do you get some sort of one-night pass?

I mean, I've had a one night stand before after a really nice dinner.

How exactly would this be any different?

While one part of me asks that question, another part is quick with the answer.

It's different because I wasn't auctioned off.

To a stranger.

To do with what he wants for the night.

That's the fucking difference.

"So, what do you think?" I ask.

"I don't know," Caroline shrugs.

I'm actually shocked by this.

Caroline likes good sex and anything fabulous.

What could be more fabulous than some hot rich guy paying double the average US annual salary to spend one night with him?

"Are you serious?" I ask. "I thought you were down for this for sure."

"Why? Because I'm such a slut?"

"No, of course, not. You know I don't think that. I just thought that you would think this is fun."

"I do," she says, hesitantly. "I'm just not sure. Just something about this...sounds strange."

I nod. It does. It is very unusual.

A girl near us waves Lizbeth over.

"I just had a question. What is the auction like? Do we just stand up there in what we're wearing now and they bid on us?" she asks.

"Well, there's an auctioneer who oversees the auction," Lizbeth says. "They stand at a podium and you stand near the auction block near them. The auctioneer organizes the bids in standardized increments of about ten thousand and the prospective buyers raise their paddle if they want to place a bid for that particular increment. As far as what you wear... you will wear what you're wearing now. The bidders do not have the right to ask you to remove any clothing or to show your breasts or anything like that. That's for later."

"Wow, that was quite a thorough explanation," I whisper to Caroline.

"Okay, ladies," Lizbeth says loudly. "If you are ready to participate, please turn your signed contracts over to me."

I look over at Caroline.

It's now or never.

It's not like we're going to do this together, but there's something comforting about having a friend go through something with you.

"I can't do this," she says quietly.

"Oh, are you sure?" I ask.

She nods confidently, placing the pen on top of the contract.

"I guess we're both going home, huh?" she asks. "What a bummer."

"Well, actually, I think I'm going to do it."

"What?!"

"I don't know," I shrug. "It's a lot of money. And the guys are pretty hot."

CHAPTER 9 - ELLIE

WHEN YOU ARE ALL ALONE AND YOU SUDDENLY REGRET
YOUR DECISION...

The fact that Caroline is leaving is making me reconsider my decision.

This whole thing was Caroline's idea and it's hard to imagine being here without her.

I follow her back to our room and watch her pack up her clothes.

"Are you sure you want to stay?" she asks.

I shrug my shoulders. I don't really know.

"Why don't you want to?" I ask.

"I don't really know," she shrugs as well. "I thought I would. I mean, when she first came out and talked about the auction, it sounded exciting. But now, I don't know. There's something about it that's just off. I mean, isn't it a little odd?"

I nod. "It's definitely not a normal thing to do."

"I mean, don't get me wrong, the guys are really attractive. And obviously rich. I just don't think I can make it up there to the podium. And what if he wants me to do something that I don't want to do?"

"Like what?" I ask.

I don't mean to be cheeky, but I wasn't aware of anything sexual that Caroline didn't do.

She has had a threesome, she had anal sex, she even went to an orgy.

I'm pretty sure that she has done everything there is to do, even tried a little bit of bondage and tying up.

I look at Caroline.

She is staring down at the floor and shuffling her feet a little.

"I just can't do this," she says.

She actually looks terrified.

Suddenly, my trepidation about my own decision starts to feel more like anxiety.

I'm not nearly as experienced as Caroline and if she's not doing this, then maybe I shouldn't be doing this either.

The whole experience reminds me a lot of going to Six Flags when I was thirteen.

I went with a good friend of mine and she was all set on riding the biggest rollercoasters.

Then she chickened out.

I was afraid to go in the first place, and after she refused to go, I was questioning my decision even more.

That time in Six Flags, I decided to go along with her.

But this time, something is keeping me here. I'm afraid and uncertain, but I can't make myself go.

"Are you sure you want to stay?" Caroline asks, one last time.

She's holding her bag and Lizbeth is at the door waiting to escort her to the helicopter.

I nod.

Lizbeth has a satisfied look on her face and a small little smile.

She knows what's about to happen and she isn't staying.

I give Caroline a brief hug and tell her that I'll see her soon.

I don't actually know how long I'm going to stay on the yacht.

Maybe I'll be back tomorrow, maybe I'll stay a few days.

This whole place is so mysterious, I'm afraid that I'm going to make a wrong move and do something improper at any moment.

When Caroline leaves, my chest seizes up.

My hands feel clammy and all blood drains from my face.

What have I done? I feel sick to my stomach and sit down on the bed to calm myself.

Did I really just stay here all alone?

How the hell am I going to get off this yacht if I do want to leave?

Is the contract really binding?

What if I watch the beginning of the auction and then I want to leave?

A million thoughts run through my mind at a speed of a thousand miles per minute.

I feel like I'm going to pass out.

I lie down on the bed and close my eyes.

A knock at the door wakes me up. I don't know how long I've been asleep.

"Come in."

A girl who was sitting across the room from me walks in.

She's tall and thin and gorgeous and looks just as terrified as I feel.

She introduces herself as Olivia.

"I'm sorry to bother you, I'm just trying to find another person who stayed."

"Really? Did not many people stay?" I ask.

"I don't think so. I tried a number of rooms before I got to yours and no one responded," Olivia says.

Wow, that does not make me feel any better.

There's another knock on the door. Lizbeth comes in and tells us that the auction is starting soon.

"What should we wear?" Olivia asks.

"You can wear what you're wearing now," Lizbeth says. "Or you can change into something more provocative. It's up to you and how you want to present yourself."

"More provocative?" I ask. I'm already wearing a hip hugging dress and heels.

"Some girls have chosen to wear only a bra and panties and some even go up there naked."

Oh my God.

My heart sinks.

What have I done?

Bra and panties?

Going stark naked in a room full of strangers?

Suddenly, I'm coming to the realization that I'm way out of my league.

The girls who do this must be made of steel and have the confidence of a rich wealthy man.

They must have gorgeous bodies without a single imperfection.

"It's really up to you," Lizbeth says, probably sensing my hesitation. "The girls have been successful wearing dresses, pants, and everything in between. You really just want to go up there and be your true self."

Yeah right, I fight the urge to roll my eyes.

When Lizbeth leaves, Olivia turns to me and says that she's going to strip down to her bra and panties.

"It's just like a swimsuit and if it fetches a better price, then why not?"

I shake my head.

"No, I can't do that," I say. "Aren't you scared, though?"

"Yes, terrified," she says, taking off her dress.

Her push up bra makes her breasts look amazing.

She's wearing a thin lacy thong on the bottom.

Her stomach is flat and almost chiseled.

"You've got an amazing body," I say.

"Thanks, you too," she says politely.

"Yeah, right," I say with a shrug.

My stomach is not really flat and I'm about five inches shorter than she is.

She seems to be all legs while my legs are kind of on the short side.

"If you feel uncomfortable, you should just wear that dress. You look amazing in it."

I nod.

That's probably what I'm going to do.

After giving myself a brief once over in the mirror, I follow Olivia back to the main cabin.

CHAPTER 10 - ELLIE

WHEN THE AUCTION STARTS…

*L*izbeth meets us in the hallway right before we come in and shuttles us out to another room.

This is the waiting room with some refreshments at the far corner of the room.

I count the girls as we wait for the auction to start.

There are ten girls there, all in various levels of undress.

About four are completely naked, sitting and chatting so comfortably as if they're wearing their pajamas.

Then there are a couple in their bra and panties, two just in panties, and two who are still dressed in dresses.

I'm one of those.

Suddenly, I feel very overdressed for the occasion, as if I had shown up to a baseball game wearing a prom dress.

The stage is right in front of us and Lizbeth positions herself at the podium.

She's going to be the auctioneer.

I peek out to get a look at the men in the room.

There are many familiar faces there including Blake Garrison and Harrison Brooks.

Some are young like them, but there are also plenty of old men too.

I've never been with anyone over thirty.

But the men in the audience aren't just old. They're really old. Fifties and sixties. Maybe even older. Grey hair and overweight. Shit. What did I expect? I mean, this is a luxury super-yacht. Not many hot men in their twenties can afford this type of party.

Lizbeth introduces herself to the audience and goes over the rules.

They are supposed to stay quiet and raise their paddles when they want to make a bid.

Once she calls out a price three times and no one goes higher, then the girl goes to that bidder.

They are expected to make out a check, money

order, or wire transfer to her choice of bank account before they are allowed to take her to their cabin.

I tap my fingers on the table nervously waiting for the auction to start.

A few minutes later, it finally starts.

Lizbeth calls out the first name.

Arabella, an excited nude girl in the back, jumps up and runs in four inch heels to the stage.

I keep waiting for her to trip, but she's an expert in those things.

When she gets to the beginning of the stage, she takes a deep breath and walks out with poise and confidence.

A bright flood light hits her body as the rest of the room goes dark.

Lizbeth introduces the girl by her name and height but doesn't say anything else about her.

Then she starts the bidding at ten thousand.

Quickly the paddles start to go up.

The price starts to climb.

When it reaches fifty thousand, Arabella smiles from ear to ear, turns around coyly and bends over.

Her legs are spread shoulder-length apart and her head bends all the way to the floor in a perfect yoga pose.

The bidding continues to climb higher.

It quickly reaches ninety thousand.

It stays there for three counts and Lizbeth yells, "Sold for $90,000 to the gentleman in the back."

I can't quench my curiosity anymore.

I go to the far corner of the stage and peak out to see who bought her.

The men in the back high-five an older guy who is clearly in his sixties.

My heart sinks.

Really?

Am I really going to have to sleep with a sixty-year-old?

But Arabella comes back to the room with her head held high.

She's over the moon by the process.

"I made forty-grand last year cleaning hotel rooms," she says to her friend. "Ninety grand, tax free, for one night of sex? Yes please!"

A meek little man with glasses and a brief case walks over to her and asks her how she wants the money.

While they do the paperwork, Lizbeth starts the auction again.

This time, she calls Olivia. Her eyes open wide and she takes a deep breath.

"Good luck," I whisper.

She fakes a smile and heads to the stage.

She's not as excited as Arabella.

But she walks out there with her head held high.

Again, Lizbeth starts the bidding at ten thousand.

That appears to be the starting point.

Unlike Arabella, she does not do anything but stand there with her hands on her hips.

She is dressed in a bra and panties and her body looks like it's covered in glitter under the spotlight.

Ten thousand dollars might not be ninety, but it's still an insane amount of money, I say to myself.

I mean, I make a third of that working all year.

So, even if I only get ten thousand, that's okay.

But no matter how much I try to convince myself, I still feel like I'm going to throw up at the prospect of going up there.

Olivia's auction goes up to eighty thousand and she's bought by a man in his forties.

When she comes back to the table, she seems satisfied by that number.

I would be too.

I think ten grand is worth sleeping with someone who is much younger than Arabella's man.

When the little man with the briefcase comes

over to Olivia, she asks if she can have the money in cash.

He says that they don't have that much on hand.

She debates whether she should get a money order or let the money be put directly into her checking account.

She's thinking about the tax repercussions.

Obviously, cash is best then she doesn't have to lose thirty percent to the government.

But who the hell wants to walk around with ninety thousand in cash around New York City?

Finally, she gives him her checking account number.

I'm so engrossed in their conversation that I don't notice that Lizbeth has started the auction again.

And she called my name!

"Ellie!" Lizbeth says again and again.

Olivia elbows me in the ribs.

I'm so caught-off guard that I don't even have time to worry about what is about to happen.

"She's calling you," Olivia says.

I nod and stand up.

Is this really happening?

I walk over to the stage. I'm a dead woman walking.

CHAPTER 11 - ELLIE

WHEN IT'S MY TURN…

The bright spotlight blinds me.

I can't see a thing in front me.

I put on a smile and stand with my hands by my sides.

Suddenly, I'm very well-aware of how much my high heeled shoes are pinching my feet.

I struggle to breathe in this tight dress, which doesn't allow my legs more than an inch of movement.

"Let's start the auction at $10,000," Lizbeth says into the microphone. "Can I get ten thousand?"

"Twenty-thousand. Thirty-thousand."

My eyes finally adjust to the brightness of the stage.

Paddles keep flying into the air as the numbers keep climbing high and higher.

"Okay, how about eighty thousand," Lizbeth says, clearly pleased with the way the auction is going.

Am I really going to go for eighty thousand?

That number floats around in my head as some unreachable goal.

Somewhere near the back of the room I spot Blake Garrison and Harrison Brooks.

They are sitting at the same table and raising their paddles each time the number jumps up.

Please, let it be one of those two, I say to myself.

At least, I already know them. And they're my age.

When the price reaches ninety-thousand, everyone else who was in the running drops off.

It's just these two.

And they keep going.

Am I really going to go for one hundred thousand dollars?

That kind of money doesn't even seem real.

"Now, just to let those of you know who are still in the running, we do have one very exclusive bidder. He is currently not in the room, but he does a proxy who is bidding for him. He is, of course, watching what's going on here and communicating with his proxy," Lizbeth says.

What? A secret bidder? Who is not in the room? What the hell is that? Who the hell is that?

"Now, how about we go up to $110,000?"

I look over and Blake and Brooks hold up their paddles.

They are determined.

Stay in this boys, I pray.

"My bidder would like to offer $150,000," the proxy bidder in the back yells out.

"Okay then. How about $150,000?"

The guys pause for a second.

Please, bid, please bid, I say to myself over and over.

I'm trying to compel them with my mind.

Finally, Brooks raises his paddle.

But Blake doesn't.

It's too much money.

"$250,000," the proxy in the back yells out.

Lizbeth looks absolutely shocked.

But she quickly catches herself and pulls herself back together.

She is a professional after all.

"$250,000 going once."

I stare at Brooks I try to push up his paddle with my mind but he shakes his head.

"$250,000 going twice."

Please, Brooks. Please do this for me, I want to scream out. You can't let me go away with this mystery bidder.

"Ellie is sold for $250,000 to Mr. Black."

Mr. Black.

That's the mystery bidder.

I've heard that name before.

It was whispered in hushed tones at the cocktail party.

And now he bought me.

Of all people.

For $250,000.

Now, that's an insane amount of money.

The rest of the auction is blur.

The man with the suitcase comes over and I pull out my wallet to give him my checking account info.

We wait, he transfers the $250,000 into my account.

The bank calls to confirm.

He talks to someone else on the phone.

Finally, the money is mine.

I log into my account on my phone and there it is.

All $250,000 of it.

What the hell?

Is this really happening.

Is this money real?

It's all so hard to believe.

When the money transfer is complete, another woman comes up to me.

She's dressed in a short black latex dress and high heels.

Her breasts are propped up so high they are basically spilling over her dress.

"I will escort you to Mr. Black's suite," she says. "Please follow me."

I want to make some conversation with her, but I can't physically open my mouth.

I feel numb all over.

I follow her all the way to the other end of the yacht.

The rooms get more and more glamorous and ostentatious the further along we go.

There's a large library to one side, filled with gorgeous leather-bound books.

I suddenly have an unstoppable urge to run away and lock myself in the library.

No, you have to be professional.

You just got paid more money than you would probably see in your whole life.

It's more than enough to pay off my four years of tuition, the taxes on the money and have some left over for a bit of fun.

It's the fun part that I try to focus on to keep myself going.

I could buy a ticket to anywhere in the world and spend a month there.

Or go to many different places.

I can go to Europe for a few months.

Or I can go traveling around South America.

This is all going to be worth it, Ellie, I say to myself.

When we reach the last door on the left, my beautiful escort opens it and lets us in.

I walk through the double doors into a gigantic double room suite.

There's a large king sized bed at the far end, in another room, through the open sliding doors.

The room where we enter is a beautiful carpeted area with a large wooden desk, couch, and chairs.

I think this is what people used to refer to as the sitting room back in the day.

Both rooms have floor to ceiling windows with a million lights streaming in.

Out on the water, the stars are so bright, they almost hurt your eyes.

"Mr. Black will be here shortly, but first I have to get you ready," my escort says.

"Get me ready? What do you mean?"

"He is very particular. He wants things just so," she says.

She walks over to the closet and opens it.

Inside, I see a bunch of perfect suits and one sheer gown with feathers along the edges.

She pulls out the gown and holds it up front of me.

"Please take off your dress," she says.

I'm caught off guard.

I mean, I knew that he bought me for the night, but dictating what I wear, somehow seems wrong.

But my escort continues to wait.

Finally, I decide to undress.

With great effort, I pull off my dress.

My stomach has all of these lines on it from the dress poking into me while I sat.

I put my arms in front of it to block her from seeing.

"Please take off your bra and panties as well," she says.

My bra and panties as well?

This is going too far!

But then again, I am going to have sex with him.

Did I really not think that for $250,000 I wouldn't be expected to take off my bra and panties?

Once I take off my bra, I kneel down to take off my shoes.

At least, there's one good thing about this. I can finally take off these pinching things.

"Please, keep your heels on," she says.

Dammit, I mutter to myself.

I peel off my panties and drop them on the chair along with my dress and bra.

My escort takes the gown off the coat hanger and helps me into it.

There is no front.

It's just a long sheer robe.

A dressing gown.

It's entirely see-through.

"Now, go and lie down on the bed," my escort says.

"On top of the sheets?" I ask.

She nods.

I find a spot in the middle, propping myself up with the pillows.

She comes over and opens the drawer on the end table.

She pulls out a long strap with a cuff at the end.

"What's that?"

"Mr. Black would like you tied up," she explains.

Tied up?

My mind begins to race.

No, no, no, I can't be tried up.

"Don't worry," she says. "It's very sexy. He isn't going to do anything to hurt you...unless you want him to."

"Why would I want him to?" I ask.

She laughs.

"Because you will. You'll be begging him to."

I understand the words that are coming out of her mouth, but I also don't.

I have no idea what she's talking about.

Why would I want him to hurt me?

I give her my one hand and watch as she puts the leather cuff around my wrist.

She then tied the strap to the bed post.

Carefully, walking around the bed, she does the same thing with my left hand.

I pull on my wrists.

No, this isn't a joke.

Both of my hands are tied to the bed posts.

My escort than leans over me and arranges my robe.

She makes sure that the feather trim covers up my breasts and other bits and then smiles at herself when she's done.

"Okay, one last thing," she says and pulls something out of her pocket.

It's a black mask.

"He doesn't want me to see him?" I ask.

My heart starts to race a mile a minute.

No, I can't have my eyes covered.

This is going too far.

"I'm sure you will later. He just doesn't want you to see him right away."

She puts the mask over my eyes.

Suddenly, I become a lot more keenly aware of every sound that exists in the room.

Somewhere in the distance, something is buzzing.

My escort exhales small shallow breaths.

The bedspread makes a rustling sound while she leans over me.

"Okay, enjoy yourself," she says and walks out of the room.

CHAPTER 12 - ELLIE

WHEN THE MASK IS ON…

I wait on the bed breathing very fast for what feels like forever. My fingers nervously fidget and run along edge of my restraints. I can't see the robe that I'm wearing, but I know it's the sexiest thing I've ever worn for a man. Plus, the feathers feel very soft and comfortable. It's like I'm wrapped in luxury.

Waiting is pure torture. There's room in the mask for my eyes to open freely without my eyelashes touching the fabric, but all I see is blackness around me. How long do I have to wait like this? My thoughts keep going back to the amount of money that the mysterious Mr. Black paid for me. $250,000. That's a lot of money. I wonder what kind of night he is expecting from all of this. To tell you the truth, I'm not the most exciting girl in bed. I'm actually quite boring. I don't like to do a lot and I'm not a huge fan of being on top. When I'm on top, I can never relax enough to actually orgasm.

The door swings open. I exhale and inhale deeply, trying to compose myself. My body suddenly gets really cold and really hot at the same time. My hormones must be going nuts. I hear the footsteps approaching the bed.

"Hello?" I ask, not able to bear the anticipation much longer.

"Good evening," he says after a moment. His voice is smooth, and deep, and has a kind of oak quality to it. He doesn't sound very old, but then again, what do I know about voices?

"Are you Mr. Black?" I ask.

"Yes, I am," he says slowly. "But you may call me Sir."

"Just sir?" I ask.

"Yes, just sir."

I don't know what he's doing, but it sounds like he's walking around the suite. At one point, the closet doors open and close. And the sound of his walk changes. It's almost as if he took off his shoes.

His footsteps are lighter, not as heavy. A moment later, I'm pretty certain that he's either barefoot or at least in socks. I chew on my lower lip nervously, my eyes are fixed on the darkness inside the mask.

Suddenly, something touches my lips. It's soft. It takes me a minute to realize that it's his finger. I listen to his easy breaths and feel his presence on top of me. Yet, the only thing that he's touching is my lips.

"It's going to be fun," he says slowly. His voice is almost smoldering now, as if a voice could be smoldering.

"I'm sorry, it's just a nervous habit of mine. I chew my lower lip a lot."

"Well, we'll have to work on that, won't we?" he says coyly.

I can't see his face or his body, and yet my body is suddenly having a very strong reaction to him. I don't know if it's his voice or him touching my lips, but my legs suddenly have these little pangs running through them. I curl my toes to try to relax, but more come. I hate to admit it, but I only feel this when I'm strongly attracted to someone. So much so that I can't control it. Just thinking about this, makes my whole body clench up for a moment.

As he hovers somewhere over me, I'm not entirely sure where, but I do feel his weight to the right of me, I feel myself shrinking. My legs press together tightly and my arms pull the restraints tightly. I'm clamming up. I'm not a particularly outgoing person. I'm a writer, for crying out loud. And my shy way of being is getting the better of me.

"Oh no, we can't have this," Mr. Black says quietly, brushing his fingers on my knees. They are raised up, and when he touches them, they fall back down to the bed without much effort. I feel myself melting like butter around him. He runs his fingers along the top of my legs and a little bit on my inner thighs. I begin to feel myself start to panic. A cold sweat runs downs my arm pits. I've never allowed a man who I wasn't involved with romantically to touch me before. And I don't even know what he looks like. I can't do this. I have to give him back his money and apologize. But I really, really can't do this.

I'm about to say this out loud, when he puts his hand gently around my neck. The feel of his skin is warm and inviting.

"You can relax. I'm not going to hurt you," he says. He runs his fingers around my clavicle and on my chest, right before my breasts he stops. I can feel my chest move up and down and his hand moves up and down along with each breath. I'm starting to relax and shut down at the same time. The intensity of this situation is getting too much, and we haven't even done anything yet.

"You can relax," he whispers into my ear. His soft breath caresses my earlobe. "I'm not going to hurt you, unless you want me too." As he says that, he presses his lips around my earlobe and kisses me lightly.

There's that phrase again. Unless I want him too. What does that mean exactly, I want to ask. But my mouth is as dry as a desert. It's almost as if he had sucked all of the moisture out of the air. Except for the moisture between my legs. I rub my legs together to try to keep the moisture where it is.

Mr. Black presses his fingertips beneath my chin, lifting my face up to him. He has a soft and demanding touch. It sends electricity through every inch of my body.

"Would you like me to kiss you?" he asks. I want to say yes. But my mind is all muddy right now.

"I don't know," I say. I have no idea why I said that.

"That's okay," he says, lowering himself next to me on the bed. "But what is not okay is for you to not call me sir."

I nod.

"Do you understand?" Mr. Black asks, running

his fingertips around the contours of my breasts, underneath my robe.

I nod again.

"You have to say out loud."

"Yes, I understand," I say.

"No, apparently, not," he says, opening the right side of my robe and exposing my breast. I feel both of my nipples getting hard. I tighten the grip on my restraints.

"Yes, I understand, sir."

"That's a good girl," he says. He continues to run his fingers in concentric circles around my nipples, not once skirting either one. The game is starting to make me crazy.

"Is there something you want?" he asks, probably sensing the disappointed look on my face.

"That just feels really good...sir."

"Oh yes, I know."

I open my mouth slightly, and let a small gasp escape from my throat. I've never been so aroused just by someone's touch before. I mean, he isn't even really doing anything. Suddenly, his hand leaves my breasts and travels back to my lips. The tip of his thumb brushes across my lower lip. He's teasing me. Toying with me. Then he presses his thumb inside my mouth and whispers, "suck."

I don't even need the command. My lips instinctively press around his thumb as my tongue strokes it.

"Mmm," he moans into my ear.

My cheeks heat up as my mouth opens and closes around his thumb inside of my mouth. I massage him with my tongue, taste his skin and realize that his fingers are soft and light. This is not the thumb that belongs to a man who works with his hands.

"There's going to be more of this to come," he says, pulling his thumb out of my mouth. "But for now…"

As he returns his fingers back to my body, I smile. I find his arrogance extremely sexy. I'm no stranger to arrogance - no one is who attends an Ivy League school. But most of the time, I find it tiresome and boring. But with Mr. Black, it is different. Authentic. Like he's not just pretending to be an arrogant prick. Like he's actually this unbelievably confident.

"Am I ever going to see your face?" I ask. "Sir."

I feel him thinking about it as he returns his attention to my breasts. His fingertips are getting closer and closer to my nipples, and the wait is excruciating.

"Yes, of course. Just not now."

"Why not, sir?"

"You know, you have a lot of questions for a girl in your position." He says laughing.

"What do you mean, sir?" I ask. It's not actually as awkward to say 'sir' at the end of each sentence. In fact, it's kind of sexy.

"Well, here you are, on my yacht. I just paid a quarter of a million dollars to spend the night with you. To do whatever I want with you and you are here making demands."

"No, not at all, sir," I say.

"See, that's exactly what I'm talking about," he says. I hear some rustling of clothing, and then something silky and soft touches my lips.

"We're going to have to bind this mouth of yours since you can't keep it closed," he says, and wraps what feels like a silk tie around my mouth.

I should be horrified and petrified by his tone and his actions. But instead, I'm incredibly turned on. I'm actually wet in between my legs. My nipples are so hard they're like little razorblades.

"We're going to take things slowly. Trust me, you're going to really enjoy yourself. But you will also need to follow my orders. You have to do anything I say, anything I ask of you. Immediately. Do you understand?"

I nod my head. My mouth again feels like a desert, but that's because all of my moisture has escaped elsewhere.

Again, he starts to run his fingers around my breasts, only this time he does touch my nipples. Soft at first and then a bit harder. He presses his lips and sucks on them a little, sending my body into uncontrollable shivers.

"You have to control yourself, Ellie. And under no circumstances can you orgasm without my permission."

What? I don't need his permission to orgasm. Do I? No, of course not. And yet, waiting for him to say it's okay, is incredibly sexy.

While his lips return to my nipples, caressing me with sucking and licking and even flicking with the tongue, his hand runs down my body. It pauses briefly near my belly button, but quickly continues its way down. The soft touch of his hands on my inner thighs, opens them up, widely.

"Oh no, not yet, my dear," he pushes my legs back together. The wetness has nowhere to go now. I can't even get it aired out. I moan a little.

"Oh are you disappointed, my dear?" he asks

with my right nipple in between his teeth. He's toying with me. Teasing me.

I nod and say yes through the fabric in my mouth.

"Well, you're going to have to get used to it."

The thought of dissatisfaction causes a shiver to run down my legs. It pools somewhere in my pelvic region. After a few minutes of caressing my breasts, he finally says, "Okay, you can open your legs now."

My legs fly open immediately. I feel exposed and on display and incredibly sexy at the same time. I'm laying myself out as an offering to him. I'm waiting for him to claim me. The thought of him coming inside of me, sends shivers down my body. I've never felt this way about anyone I've never seen before. But right now I'm not thinking. I'm feeling. I'm existing entirely on another plane of existence - one that's made entirely of emotions.

He runs his hands around my thighs and around my belly button. Then he makes his way down to my thighs. He starts at the knees and goes up. I hear him lick his lips and I feel his eyes looking at my body. Admiring it. His fingers suddenly run upward, and trace a slow path in between my breasts and down to my stomach. I close my eyes under the mask and moan. His hands are so soft that his touch feels like little butterfly kisses. The whole experience is not only sexual, it's also incredibly sensual.

I relax against the restraints and allow myself to drift away into a fantasy. I feel him deep within me and my thighs start to move accordingly. I pretend that we have known each other forever, but this is the first time that we're having sex. Suddenly, his touch gets more and more intense. His hands wrap around my legs and I realize how big his hands really are. Much bigger than they seemed from the touch of his fingers.

He takes the trim of my bathrobe and runs it over my stomach. The bottom half of my body moans in ecstasy and I close my legs to try to push some of it away.

"Oh no, we can't have you doing this," Mr. Black says, pushing my legs apart. My heart jumps into my throat and starts to beat extremely fast.

Then he takes the feather trim and runs it across my clitoris. It almost screams out for more. He runs the feathers along my thighs and then around my vagina. The lips open up for more and he laughs. Then he kneels down in front of my opened thighs and blows on me.

"Oh my God," I mumble into the tie around my mouth.

"Now, remember, you promised. You're not going to orgasm without me saying so, are you?"

"No, sir" I mumble. Though at this point, I'm actually getting very close. Usually, it takes me a long time to orgasm. I'm not naturally a very sexual person. But there's something about Mr. Black that just makes me wet. There's no other way, no other more delicate way, of putting it.

After putting the feathers back to my sides, he positions himself right in front of my opened thighs. Oh my God. Here it is. He's going to kiss me. Or stick a finger in me. He's going to do something to release all this amazingly horrible pleasure that has been building up within me.

But much to my surprise, I hear a quiet vibrating sound come on instead. And then it touches me. My clitoris. A sharp cry of pleasure-pain seizes through my body as the vibrating sensation spreads through me. I find myself intoxicated with this new kind of roughness. My legs open further and reach up, as my inhibitions seem to fall by the wayside.

"That's a good girl," Mr. Black says. "How does this feel?"

"Amazing," I mumble.

Suddenly, the vibrating sensation stops and the sound disappears.

"Now, what did I say about calling me sir? If you don't do what I say, you don't get the pleasure that I'm wanting to give you," he says.

"It feels amazing, sir," I mumble quickly. "Please don't stop, sir. Please, sir."

He presses the vibrator back to me, only this time it goes into my vagina, and he starts the vibrations. The vibrations are faster this time, making me nearly choke up on my breaths.

"You're a very sexy girl, Ellie," Mr. Black says. "I think you deserve something extra for being so sexy."

"Thank you, sir," I mumble, floating away on pangs of pleasure.

And just when I thought I couldn't feel any better, suddenly, I feel his breath on my clit. He inhales deeply. And then exhales. And he presses his soft, almost liquid tongue on top of it. I feel my back arch off the bed and my body presses up to fill his mouth even more. He moans approvingly, pushing the vibrator deeper inside of me.

"That's it, beautiful. Show me what you're made of," he whispers and begins to suck on it more aggressively.

"Oh my God. I'm getting so close, sir" I say,

feeling that warm sensation running up my legs. My toes have already gone numb.

"Tell me, when you're about to come," he says. I nod.

"There, there, sir" I start to moan and I feel like I'm just about to climax.

And suddenly, everything stops. He pulls his mouth away from me and turns off the vibrator.

"Not now, Ellie," he says coyly.

Wait, what? I don't understand. My legs flop down onto the bed in disappointment.

"You can't come so soon, honey," he says, running his fingers over my breasts. "The night is young. We are just getting started."

My mind starts to swim. I don't understand anything he's saying. It takes me a few minutes to feel okay again. My heartbeat slowly returns to normal. My body temperature slowly drops and I start to feel cold. I've never felt so dissatisfied before.

CHAPTER 13 - ELLIE

WHEN THE MASK COME OFF...

*a*fter Mr. Black pulls out of me without letting me get off, I feel angry. Really angry. Who the hell does he think he is? Why the fuck is he toying with me? He might have paid for me for the night, but that doesn't mean anything. I'm a free woman and he has no right to do this to me.

"What the fuck are you doing?" I ask. I must've caught him off guard, because he doesn't respond for a few moments. I wish my arms weren't tied up anymore, so I could take off this damn mask.

"Excuse me?" he asks. The tone of his voice changes. It drops about an octave.

"Why didn't you let me get off?" I ask.

"Because...this is just the beginning."

"Or maybe it's the end," I say. I'm sulking. Upset.

I guess this is what men refer to as blue balls, because I'm livid. My cheeks are actually burning with anger.

He leans over me. I cower away from him. Get the fuck away from me you asshole, I want to say. But when he takes the tie from my mouth and takes off my blindfold, I'm glad that I kept my mouth shut.

The lights in the room have been dimmed, making the place look like it has been lit up by candlelight. When my eyes focus on Mr. Black, I'm taken a little bit by surprise.

I don't know what I was expecting, but for some reason I thought that he might be wearing some leather.

Being tied up isn't full on bondage, of course, but he was clearly into it and isn't that what BDSM is about?

From what I've seen on the internet, the dress code seems to be quite important to the community.

But Mr. Black is dressed in an impeccably tailored suit. I wouldn't be surprised if it cost a couple of grand and was by some sort of fancy designer. It's dark-gray and the pants are tailored with a snug fit that accentuates his lean muscular legs. He is tall and broad-shouldered and I immediately try to imagine him in the nude. What does he look like under all those clothes? My eyes slowly drift up to his face.

"Are you going to untie me?" I ask.

He smiles out of the corner of his mouth.

"You're kind of a feisty one, aren't you?"

"Listen, I may have signed a contract to anything sexually, but you clearly didn't want to finish what you started. So that part is over...for now."

Who is this talking? Are these my words coming out of my mind? There is something about being tied up that's making me incredibly confident. And cocky. Usually, I'm the girl who is cowering in the corner, but now I feel like I am the most powerful woman in the world.

"So, are you going to untie me?" I ask again. This time, I use an even more forceful voice.

As Mr. Black glides over to the bed - he does not walk like normal men, no, he glides - I glance into his impossibly blue-green eyes. They are a perfect compliment to his tan, sun kissed skin. Shivers run up my spine. Mr. Black looks dangerous and I like it. He takes his time untying my hands, occasionally looking over at me. When our eyes meet, it takes all of my strength not to look away. But I'm done cowering. And he's done having the upper hand in all of this.

Once my hands are free, I rub my wrists and ask
him where the bathroom is. He points me to the
room on the other side of the suite. The bathroom is
all tile and has a very high ceiling like the rest of the
suite. I've been on sailboats before, but only small
thirty-footers, with ancient wooden paneling and
crammed interiors. I've never been on a boat this
big. Come to think of it, it's actually hard to believe
that this is a boat at all. The yacht is so large that you
can barely feel that it's moving at all. The only
indication that you have that it's a boat at all is the
360-degree views of the blue water out of each
window.

I lean over the marble vanity and look at myself
in the mirror. The sheer robe with the feather trim is
quite becoming. The feathers hide all of the
imperfections and make me feel very luxurious and
incredibly sexy. I kneel down and flip my hair a
couple of times. Laying on my back for so long,
made it fall flat a bit and I want to infuse it with a
little bit more body.

Next, I check my eye makeup. My eyeliner is a
little smeared on the right eye, giving it an
unintended smoky eye look. I wipe some of it off and
flash myself a smile. I'm usually not this vain. In fact,
I hardly care about makeup and frilly clothes at all.

But there's something about Mr. Black and this yacht that makes me want to try.

What the hell are you doing, Ellie? I ask silently, looking at myself in the mirror. This whole scene isn't you. If it's anyone, it's Caroline, but it was too much for even her. Why are you really here? There's of course the usual answer. I owe over one hundred and fifty thousand dollars in student loans. And while they won't pay themselves, Mitch and my mom are more than happy to cover the expenses. Christ, they didn't even want me to take out any loans. So, why did I? Pride. It's this stubborn, middle-class pride that I must've inherited from my father, who also famously refuses to take any money from my mom. But at least my dad has an excuse, she's his ex-wife.

Still, there is something to be said for paying your own way. I know that I'm not paying my own rent, but I am paying for everything else. I've always thought that it would really mean something if I was actually able to pay off my student loans on my own. Maybe it would mean that I'm actually a success. That I've actually made something of myself as a writer.

And when this opportunity came up...I don't know, it just felt right. But more than that, it felt exciting. And besides being a stubborn, stick-in-the-mud, I'm also not the type of girl to do a lot of exciting things. For crying out loud, I never even tried pot in high school because I was too much of a wimp. I hardly took a sip of beer until I was eighteen. I've never let myself go in anything. I wanted to audition for the school play my senior year, but I chickened out. I wanted to go away on a study abroad semester, but again I was too much of a coward. I'm not very old, but I've lived a very sheltered life. Mostly, because of my own decisions. So, when this auction came about, I decided that I've had enough. Enough of being scared. Enough of not taking chances. Enough of not living my life to the fullest.

"Are you okay in there?" Mr. Black asks through the door. Suddenly, I realize that I've been in the bathroom for a very long time.

"Yes, I'll be out in a minute."

I look in the mirror one last time. I don't know what's in store for me for the rest of the night, but at least I'm doing something unexpected. I'm living life on the edge. I'm jumping off a cliff without a parachute. What can be more exciting that?

I walk out of the bathroom with my head held high. I straighten out my shoulders and flash Mr.

Black a mischievous smile. He's standing in front of the large circular table in the middle of the living room suite with a Champagne bottle in one hand and two glasses in another.

"I thought that some Champagne might be in order," he says. As I make my way over to the table, I see the large bowl of bright red strawberries.

"Those look good."

"Yes, they are. Organic. Freshly picked from a farmer's market."

I'm somewhat of a lover of fruit. And if they're actually from a farmer's market, and they look that beautiful, they must've cost $10 a pound. Champagne on the other hand is something I don't really know very well. But given where we are and who Mr. Black is, I doubt that it's from the discount aisle.

He pops the bottle and fills two glasses. Then he sits down and looks at me.

"Why don't you have a seat right here?" he asks, patting his thigh. There are plenty of places to sit all around, but I comply. I find his confidence, that's bordering on arrogance, intoxicating.

When I sit down on his thigh and make myself comfortable, the first thing I feel is the bulge in his crotch. It's rather big and I'm rather pleased by that fact. The size of the penis doesn't really make much difference to me. However, it is nice to know that everything about Mr. Black is in proportion, starting with his huge yacht, his enormous suite, and ending with his gorgeous face, lean broad-shouldered body, and his substantial package. It's good to know that all of this money and wealth isn't just some way of compensating for certain shortcomings.

After I'm in place on his lap, Mr. Black dunks a strawberry in the glass of Champagne.

"Open wide," he instructs. When the strawberry, covered in cold bubbles, brushes along my lower lip, shivers run up my entire body and a warm sensation starts to build somewhere in between my legs. I bite into the strawberry and marvel at the sweetness as it runs down my throat.

"Mmm-mmm," I say, licking my lips. Before I get the chance to finish the strawberry, a small drop of Champagne falls on my collarbone. I'm about to wipe it with my hand, when Mr. Black brushes them away and presses his lips to my skin. After kissing me lightly, he then licks my skin and sucks on it with a little force. I toss my head back and close my eyes, to enjoy the moment.

"Mmm-mmm," I say. "That's even better."

After kissing my collarbone and neck, he takes a

sip of his champagne.

"So, I've been meaning to ask you something," I say.

He looks at me and waits for the question.

"What's your name?"

"I thought you knew my name."

"Well, I know you as Mr. Black," I say.

"That's what you can call me," he says and takes another sip.

Is he for real? I stare at him but my glares don't seem to faze him one bit. Suddenly, I feel like a total idiot. What am I doing here if the man won't even tell me his real name?

"Listen, I don't mean to be rude, but we don't really know each other very well. I mean, I'd like to change that. But for now, please just call me Mr. Black," he says. The tone of his voice is more appeasing and apologetic, but I'm not satisfied.

"And one more thing," he adds with a smile and a twinkle in his eye. "Don't forget to refer to me as Sir."

I nod, not really knowing how to respond to him. He's both flirting and demanding of me. A part of me is insulted. How dare he speak to me that way? Who does he think he is? But another part, knows that it's just a game. I'm his for the night and if he wants me to call him Sir for a quarter million dollars, then why not? What's the big deal?

"Here, I have a surprise for you," he says and picks up a remote control even though there isn't a television in sight. He points it at the curtains across from us. Pressing the button, the curtains swing open.

Expecting to see the wide dark ocean and a starry sky, I am genuinely taken aback by the show that's taking place before my very eyes. Shocked, actually. There, on a bit of a raised stage, behind glass as if they are in an aquarium, are three people in various levels of undress. There are three people, two girls and a guy, who are all having sex with one another.

"You like?" Mr. Black asks.

I look at the stage and then at Mr. Black and then back at the stage. I actually don't know how to respond to this. I've never seen anything like this before. I get up for a closer look. There are three of them. The blonde girl is dressed in a pink bra and crotch-less panties. The brunette is on all fours and kissing the blonde's breasts and then going down on her. The toned, bronzed blonde guy with the physique of a Greek god, kissing the brunette's tight ass and slowly inserting his finger inside of her.

"What is this?" I ask.

"It's a private show. Something to get us in the mood."

I didn't realize that we needed to get in the mood. Though, I hate to admit it but I am suddenly keenly aware of how aroused I am.

"I've never seen anything like this," I say.

"Yes, not many people have. It's not exactly like watching porn, is it?" Mr. Black asks.

I shake my head. No, it's not. It's so much more real. There's a real authenticity to the group. I mean, they are actually here. Right before us. Doing things to each other. I look closer at their faces to try to see if any of them look familiar.

"You didn't meet them at the party," Mr. Black says. "They are performers not guests."

"Performers?" I ask.

"Yes." He shrugs nonchalantly. "This is what they do for a living. They are hired by very exclusive private parties as performers. They only have sex with each other and they have the whole thing very choreographed and practiced so that it's always exciting to watch."

Sex performers? Besides strippers and escorts, I've never heard of this particular type of sex performance. Wow, what a world.

Mr. Black pulls over two large soft chairs, which look much more comfortable than the ones around the dining room table. He positions them right in front of the window.

"Come here," Mr. Black pats the seat next to him. "Don't overanalyze this. Let's just enjoy."

I sit down in my chair and look up at the stage. The brunette is on all fours with her tongue in the blonde's pussy. The guy is having sex with her from behind. A few minutes later, he pulls out and goes over to the blonde. She licks him and goes down on him while the brunette uses a large vibrator on her, making her scream with pleasure.

"Are you turned on?" Mr. Black asks.

I nod, making the understatement of the century. I've never been this turned on. I cross and uncross my legs to try to get the warming sensation to go away, but it doesn't. He had teased me enough, gotten me to the edge and now any thought, let alone a real life visual takes me back to full arousal.

Suddenly, I can't keep my hands to myself anymore. I start to rub my breasts lightly and my hands run down my body without asking for my consent or permission. When I touch my clit and reach further inside of myself, I know immediately that this won't take long.

"Hey, hey, hey!" Mr. Black turns to me, pulling my hand out of me. He takes my fingers and licks them carefully, one by one, and then looks straight into my eyes. "What do you think you're doing?"

"This is very arousing, Sir."

"Yes, I know," he says with a coy smile. "But you can't orgasm yet. Not without my permission."

I stare at him, not entirely understanding the words that are coming out of his mouth.

"Well, do you want to have sex then?" I ask. "Sir?"

"Oh no, honey, tonight won't be that easy."

"I don't understand, Sir."

"You are mine for the night, Ellie. And that means I tell you when and where you will orgasm. Right now, we're just building anticipation."

I shake my head.

"Disappointed?" he asks, flashing his pearly whites at me.

"I've already built anticipation, Sir."

"Oh yes, I can see that. And taste that."

I return my eyes to the stage and try to focus on something else. But all I see before me is the thing that brings me back to the thing that apparently I can't do. The brunette is laying on her back with the blonde on top of her on all fours. They are each eating each other out while the guy goes back and forth between getting a blow job and having sex with one and then the other. My yearning gets mixed up with anger and disappointment and, frankly, I don't know how to deal with it.

I glance over at Mr. Black. His eyes are transfixed on the stage as well. I decide that this is my chance. Maybe I can do this and be very quiet. I take my left hand, the one that's furthest away from him, and slowly slide it under my butt. Much to my surprise, I don't even have to put it in very far. Suddenly, an overwhelming warm sensation floods my whole body and I moan from pleasure.

When I get control of my senses, I open my eyes and see Mr. Black's eyes staring at me.

"I'm sorry, Sir," I say quietly. "I just couldn't help it."

Mr. Black shakes his head, disapprovingly. I don't know him well enough to know whether he is secretly pleased or not.

"Well, then, Ellie," he says slowly. "You've been a very bad girl. And you know what happens to bad girls?"

"No, Sir."

"They get punished."

CHAPTER 14 - ELLIE

WHEN I GET PUNISHED…

$\mathcal{I}$ didn't know what getting punished meant, but I was secretly excited to see that disapproving look on his face. There was something about the way he said it. It sent chills through my whole body.

Mr. Black got out of his chair and walked over to the bed.

"Come here," he instructed me. The tone of his voice sent chills through my body. Suddenly, I got even more excited than I was before. What the hell was he going to do to me for doing this? I couldn't wait to find out.

"Take off your robe."

I hesitate for a moment. This whole time, my feather-trimmed robe has been my protector. My shield. And now, I had to remove it and stand here naked before him in all of my glory.

"Take off your robe," he says. "Or I'll take it off for you."

I consider the option. Maybe I should just make him do it. But in the end, I chicken out. I open the robe and let it fall to the floor.

"Get on the bed on all fours," he says. "Facing the headboard."

After I'm in position, he comes over with more restraints. I watch as he snaps on leather cuffs around my ankles, before he ties the black ribbons attached to the cuffs to the bed post. I lay down flat on my stomach as he does this, but he prompts my butt up in the air, making sure that my ass and pussy are fully exposed. Then he snaps on leather cuffs around my wrists and ties those to the bedposts as well. The restraints are pulled tight, but not so tightly that I'm flat on my stomach.

Mr. Black slowly walks around the bed.

"You've been a bad girl, Ellie," he says. I nod.

"Have you been a bad girl?"

"Yes, I have, Sir," I whisper. Shivers are running down my body and a warming sensation pools in between my thighs. Mr. Black runs his fingers over my back, and gives my ass cheek a little slap. Then he walks over to the side, and cups my breasts. My hard-rock nipples gently fall into his hands. He massages them gently and then a little harder. He squeezes my nipples in between his fingers, taking me somewhere to the border of pain and pleasure.

Then he makes his way to my thighs. I've never been in this position in front of a man before. It's not even the fact that I'm tied, but that I'm so exposed and on display. I try to put all of that aside and stay in the moment.

Mr. Black runs his finger around my butt cheeks and my inner thighs, toying with me. He makes large concentric circles. Quickly, they become smaller and smaller ones. He's focusing his energy on my vagina and clitoris, but he isn't touching either. He's flirting with me, teasing me. I'm not sure how much more of this I can stand. And then suddenly, he presses his finger into my ass. I feel him going deeper and deeper and the sensation is overwhelming. He blows a little on my exposed and aroused labia, but does not touch, making me want to scream.

"Oh my God," I moan over and over.

Suddenly, he gives me a little lick. His rough tongue runs over my clitoris, briefly going inside of me, while his finger continues to move around in my ass. The sensation is so overwhelming that I feel like

I'm going to pass out. I feel myself dripping on his lips.

"Look to the stage," he says. I open my eyes and turn my head toward the stage. The scene looks very much like ours, except that no one is tied up. The brunette is also on all fours, with the guy's finger in her ass and his lips on her vagina.

Seeing what is being done to me being done to someone else completely overwhelms me. I feel myself reaching climax. Suddenly, my legs cramp up and my body starts to go into convulsions. I have no control over anything including how loud I scream. When I start to climax, Mr. Black follows my body's rhythms. He speeds up as I speed up, and I ride a long wave of pleasure until I collapse onto the bed.

"That was really good," I say after I come back to my senses a little bit. "I can't feel my legs."

"Good," Mr. Black says with a smile and starts to untie my restraints.

―――――

MR. BLACK OPENS the room service menu and asks me what I want. We're sitting around the dining room table and the sex show curtain is closed. Given the mind blowing orgasm, I'm still a little muddled in my head. I can't quite decide so he orders the Caesar salad and grilled salmon for both of us.

"So, tell me about yourself, Ellie," he says while we wait.

I tell him about Yale and my job at BuzzPost.

"Do you like working there?"

"Yes, it's okay. But I sort of want to do more writing. Right now, I mainly just make up quizzes and fun content, but I really want to be a writer.

"What do you write?"

"Right now, I write mainly short stories. Some essays about my life."

"Will you write about this?"

That takes me aback for a second. "What do you mean?"

"Well, this is quite an adventure, isn't it? Going to a luxury yacht party and then being auctioned off to a man you've never seen before."

"If I wrote this, this story would have a lot of sex in it."

"Yes, but sex sells," Mr. Black says.

"Would you mind if I wrote about you?"

"Oh no, not at all. People already write and print a lot of lies about me. It would be refreshing to actually have something true out there."

I stare at him. I don't really know what he means.

"You don't know who I am, do you?" Mr. Black asks, flashing me a crooked, mischievous smile.

I shrug. I really don't.

"I'm the founder and CEO of Owl. We're the leading competitor to Amazon."

"Oh, I didn't know that," I say.

"That's okay. It's nice actually. It's not every day that I meet a person who doesn't already have some preconception about me and what I'm like."

I nod as if I understand. But I really don't. I really wish I had my phone right now so I could Google him. Who is he really? What is this reputation that he's talking about?

A knock at the door breaks up my train of thought. Our food has arrived. I dig into it as soon as the delivery man leaves. After a night of all that emotion and pleasure, I'm starving.

"So, how did you get started in your line of work?" I ask.

"Eh, I always loved computers. Girls didn't really like me so I just spent all of my time in the basement building computers and writing code. I went to Yale as well, but dropped out when I first started Owl. My junior year."

It turns out that Mr. Black was at Yale exactly ten

years before me. I look him up and down as he carefully cuts his salmon.

"You don't really seem like a guy who girls wouldn't like."

"You'd be surprised. I didn't always look like this. I never worked out in high school and I was this tall scrawny kid who just knew too much about video games and not much else."

"So, if I were to google you, what else would I find out?" I ask.

"That I've been linked to a lot of models and actresses over the last seven years. That I like to have large, lavish parties that cost way too much money. Maybe I'm just trying to compensate for the fact that I couldn't get a date to my high school prom so I never went."

I really like Mr. Black's authenticity. He's so honest about himself and his past. He is also not a stranger to psychoanalysis and is quite self-aware. From what I've learned, that's quite a rare thing in a man. Even if some of them are self-aware like this, very few would actually come out and put it all out there. Especially, with a stranger.

"Can I ask you something?" he asks. I nod.

"Have you ever been tied up before?"

"No, never," I shake my head.

"But you seemed to really enjoy yourself."

I think about this for a moment chewing my salad. "Actually, I did. There was something about being completely restrained and not being able to move that made the whole thing feel very freeing. It's almost as if I could finally let myself go."

"That's good," Mr. Black smiles. "Not everyone enjoys it but those who do, really get off on it."

"Oh, are you talking about me?" I ask, jokingly.

"Yes, I definitely got that impression."

Taking a sip of wine, I take a moment to think about what he had just said. I've never tried anything like that before. It was definitely a new experience. But it was also a very hot and erotic experience. Sensual. Mind blowing. It was hard to think about all the adjectives that would describe it without reliving it. There was something about being restrained that really turned me on. I had to give myself to this man and put a lot of trust in him. But it wasn't just the trust. Surprisingly, the most freeing thing about being tied up was the fact that you suddenly feel completely free to be yourself. There's no posing. No pretending. As a woman, you are, a lot of times, the entertainment when it comes to the bedroom. You are the one who is on top or doing a lot of the work. But tonight, I had to be perfectly still. I couldn't really move. And it forced me to relax and really dive into my pleasure unlike I ever had before. There is no other word for it. It was liberating.

"So, what are you going to do with all that money?" Mr. Black asks, opening another bottle of wine. We've had two glasses each and I feel like I'm floating on air.

"I don't really know," I shrug. "I haven't given it much thought."

"It's a lot of money."

"Yes, I know. You want to make sure that I use it wisely?"

"Wisely? Are you kidding?" he laughs, tossing his hair back. I can see the muscles peek out a little bit through his jacket, and I wonder if I'm going to see him fully naked, in the flesh, today.

"What do you mean?"

"You may be surprised to learn this about me, Ellie, but I don't really care about money."

"Well, that's because you have a lot of it," I say.

"Yeah, you'd think that. But I never really cared about money. I grew up in a two bedroom one bath house with my parents and my little brother. My parents weren't poor, but we were not rich by any standard. And even back then, money never really interested me much."

"So, how did you end up so rich?"

"I went after what I was interested in. I spent all of my time with computers and I started a company in college. I didn't start it to make myself rich. I did it because it was what I was genuinely interested in. I'd be doing it if it only grew to $100,000 in revenue or $1 million."

I don't really buy it. I've met plenty of Mitch's friends and colleagues who make the same statements while paying mortgages on their three bedroom apartments on Park Avenue and their seven bedroom summer houses in the Hamptons. It's my experience that rich people like to pretend that they aren't interested in money, when in reality that's pretty much all that they're interested in.

"So, what about all this? Why do you have a multi-million dollar yacht if you say you don't care about money?" I ask.

"Oh, I never said that I didn't enjoy the perks that money affords. That's the thing about money. I think it's useless just sitting around in a bank account doing nothing. Life's short and you never know how long you have on this earth? So, why not live it up?"

I smile. "So, let me get this straight. You don't

want me to be wise with the money that I got from the auction?"

"No, I don't. I want you to be very unwise. I want you to go out there and get something extravagant that you have always wanted but could never afford. I want you to embrace the money for what it is - something that gives you pleasure."

I shake my head.

"What?" he asks, pushing a strand of hair out of my face. Shivers run up my spine when he touches me and I shudder.

"I don't think I can do that," I say. "The main reason why I participated in the auction was that I wanted my student loans to be paid off. I didn't want to take the money from my stepfather and I wanted to take care of them myself."

"How much do you owe?"

"One hundred and fifty thousand," I say. "And I make about thirty thousand and live in lower Manhattan. So, without the auction, I'd be paying off that loan for a very, very long time."

He thinks about that for a second.

"Okay, but what are you going to do with the money that's left over?" he asks after a moment. "You'd still have one hundred grand left if you write Yale a big ol' check for the rest."

"I don't owe the money to Yale, but to Sallie Mae," I flash him a smile. "But I see your point. Um, I don't really know what to do with the rest. Probably just put it in savings for a rainy day. It rains a lot in New York."

"You don't even want to take a trip somewhere exotic? It doesn't have to be expensive. You could go backpacking in Belize. You can go live for a few months in Barcelona. Or Rome."

"And what would I do there?" I ask.

"You could write," he says, without taking a pause. Suddenly, in this moment, I realize that I've never had another person see me like Mr. Black sees me. He sees through all my bullshit and posturing down to the core of who I really am.

"But I have my job," I mumble quietly.

"But then you wouldn't need it, would you?"

I shrug. I was so lucky to just get this job after graduation that I have a hard time imagining quitting it for no other reason than money. I mean, I want to write, of course. I want to write what I want to write and this money would definitely give me the freedom to do just that. But can I actually just go out there and quit the best job that I could get? I mean, what would I do when the money runs out?

"Tell me what you're thinking," Mr. Black says, lifting my chin up with his hand.

I repeat everything that just occurred to me. I tell him every insecurity and trepidation that I have without pausing for a moment.

"Well, by the time the money runs out, you'll have something written, right?" he asks.

I shrug. "I don't know. It's not so easy. I mean, I have a lot of doubts. About myself. About my dedication and my ability to write."

"Let me tell you something, Ellie," he says. "Let me tell you something that I have learned getting to where I have gotten. There are a lot of entrepreneurs out there with startup companies. We're a dime a dozen. It's a cutthroat business, not so unlike the writing business. When I first got started, I had my doubts too. But I also knew that there was nothing else that I wanted to do. Frankly, there was nothing else that I could do. So, I had to believe in myself. I had to give this a shot. And not just a shot. I had to do it until I could tell all of those people who told me that I needed a backup plan, that they're full of shit. If you have a backup plan then you'll end up doing your backup plan and not commit yourself fully to what you need to do. To succeed in anything, you have to do it 100%. And to succeed in a creative career, you have to do it until…"

"Until what?" I ask.

"You have to do it until all of your competition falls away. You do it longer than any other people. You do it despite the failures. You do it despite the setbacks. Failures and setbacks are what make other people drop out and that's good for you. Because you keep doing it until it works out. That's the only mindset you can have."

"But what if I'm not good?" I ask.

"That doesn't matter. If you enjoy writing, you will find your niche. It may be journalism, it may be fiction, it may be short stories, it may be romance or thrillers. And the other important ingredient besides determination is confidence. No one is going to believe you unless you believe in you. So, if you have to start the day with affirmations, telling yourself that you can and will become a writer, or better yet, that you are already a writer, then that's what you have to do. Success starts with a mindset and everything else follows from hard work."

I nod and try to take that all in. I know in my heart that what he is saying is right and true, but my mind is having a hard time processing it. Accepting it.

Suddenly, as if he can read my thoughts, Mr. Black leans over and pokes me in my chest with his index finger.

"You have to believe in yourself right here," he says. "And everything else will follow."

CHAPTER 15 - ELLIE

My feelings for Mr. Black undergo a change. What was just pure physical attraction and arousal suddenly changes and becomes something deeper and stronger. What is this thing that I'm feeling? Without my consent, my thoughts go back to Tom. I don't really know why he pops into my head, except that I've been in love with him for a very long time. It was always from a distance and, as a result, there was always a separation between us. But thinking about Tom now, in the presence of Mr. Black, I almost want to laugh. The infatuation that I felt for him was nothing in comparison to what I feel now. I feel actually drawn to Mr. Black. Like I have to have him and I'll scream if I don't. But I don't just have to have him sexually. I also want him emotionally. Oh shit. This could be bad.

I watch as he walks over to the bar and pours himself a whiskey. He asks if I want one, but I decline.

This is very, very wrong, Ellie. You can't let yourself be swept off your feet by him. He's a man who runs a large multinational company and owns a yacht and who knows what else. Be kind to yourself and protect your heart. He probably just wants you for the night and that's it.

"Why did you bid on me?" I ask. I don't know what made me ask that question at this moment except that maybe it'll give me an idea of how he really feels about me.

"I saw you when you first boarded the yacht. And at the cocktail party. You were not like the other girls there. I was drawn to you immediately," he says without hesitation.

"Is that why you sent me that dress to wear?"

"Yes," he nods. "I find it intoxicating telling women what to wear."

I sigh. There it is again. Women. He didn't just want to dress me. He likes to dress women. No, I can't get more emotionally involved with him than I already am. And it would be better to get a little bit less involved. This is not the type of man who can ever give me what I want.

"What's wrong, Ellie?" he asks.

I shrug.

"Nothing. I don't know," I say. And then before I have the chance to tape my mouth shut, I blurt out, "I just feel different being here with you. Different than I've ever felt."

Shut the fuck up, Ellie. What the hell are you doing? What's going to happen next? You're going to tell him that you think you might be falling in love with him? You just met him!

"Different how?" he asks.

I look away. "Different in a good way. But also kind of a scary way, I guess. I mean, I don't really know anything about you."

"What would you like to know?" Mr. Black asks.

Your name, for one, I want to say. But I bite my tongue. He already made it clear that he does not want me to know that.

"Have you ever been married?" I ask.

"Yes."

I'm taken aback by his frankness. I was definitely not expecting that answer. Mr. Black does not put off a married vibe. He definitely seems like a lifelong bachelor, but I guess maybe not.

"What happened?" I ask.

He pauses for a moment and looks down at the table and then back into my eyes.

"I usually don't tell anyone this," he says. I flash him a smile and wait.

"I got married in college. We dated for two years and one day I just asked her to marry me. It was all very spontaneous and romantic."

"Sounds like it. So, what happened?"

"I don't know. We just went to city hall one afternoon and did it. But then things started to go wrong. She said she felt guilty that we didn't have a big wedding and didn't invite all of our friends and family. Then she said she needed time off and went home to Ohio. Not long after that, she called me up and said that she wanted a divorce because she was having a baby with her high school boyfriend."

I can see the pain on his face as he tell me the story. He can't meet my gaze and when he finally looks up, he wipes a small teardrop that runs down the outside of his cheekbone.

"That was the most difficult thing I've ever experienced," Mr. Black says. "And I've never told anyone about it before. Not even a shrink."

I lean over and wrap my arms around his strong, powerful shoulders. On the outside he looks like a completely put-together man that nothing fazes. But now I've seen a glimpse of the truth. There are so many layers to him and I've just started to uncover them all.

"So, why did you tell me?" I ask. He shrugs, shying away again.

"I don't really know. But there's something about you Ellie. I just feel like I can tell you anything, my deepest darkest secrets, and it would all be okay."

"You can," I whisper into his ear.

I look at his face, examining every angle and pore. I admire the angle of his lips and the strength in his jaw. I brush away the few strands of hair that fall into his eyes.

"So, what about you? Have you ever been married?" he asks.

I laugh and shake my head.

"Have you ever been close?"

"No, not at all. For the last few years, I've been in love with a friend of mine, but he is engaged to someone else."

Oh shit. There's that word. Love. That may be the truth, but I don't know why I said that out loud. To Mr. Black of all people. It's not something that another guy wants to hear.

"That can be difficult," he says after a moment. "Unrequited love."

"Um, I don't really know if it was love or not. I mean, maybe it was just some sort of infatuation."

"Isn't that the funny thing about love?" Mr. Black asks. "It's not until you start to feel something stronger that you realize that what you felt before wasn't love at all."

I've never thought of it that way. But I guess he's right. You only have the experiences that you have and it's not until new experiences replace them that you gain the knowledge of what you were truly experiencing.

"So, let me ask you something else, Ellie," Mr. Black asks. "What's your biggest fear?"

I don't really know how to answer that. Does he mean a fear like heights or the fear of never really becoming a writer? Or the fear that I will never really fall in love and have someone love me back?

"It can be anything really," he says. "We all have fears."

"Why do you ask?"

"Because I have a theory. I believe that what we are afraid of is the thing that we have to pursue in life because our fears give us insight into who we are."

"So, you think that people who are afraid of public speaking should become public speakers?"

"Yes, probably. They are afraid of it for a reason and once they identify why that is and conquer their fear then they will be so much better as not only human beings, but also as individuals."

That's one way of thinking about it, I'll give him that.

"I'm afraid of a lot of things actually," I say quietly. "But I don't like talking about those things."

He nods as if he understands.

"Why not?" he asks.

"I don't know...I guess, they make me feel like I'm naked or something."

A coy smile comes over his face.

"I have an idea," Mr. Black says. "Why don't we get into bed and you take off your robe and tell me what you're afraid of it."

The thought of that sends shivers up my spine.

"No, I can't do that."

"You've done a lot more than that already."

"I know, but this is...private."

"No, it's not private. It's something you're afraid of. Let's just try it?"

I look into his eyes. There's an honesty and truth in them that I've never seen before in another human being. A part of me thinks this is a crazy thing to do and is resisting full on. But another parts asking, 'what if.' What if I did this? Would it be so horrible? Suddenly, my heart starts to beat faster. The thought of doing it makes me anxious, but in a good way. Excited.

I walk over to the bed and remove my robe. I drop it to the floor and climb in. Mr. Black follows me there and gets in on the other side.

I'm laying completely nude before him, while he is still dressed in his perfectly tailored suit and tie. He's even still wearing shoes and his jacket. And yet, something about laying here before him, puts me at ease. There is no judgement. His eyes are full of adoration and love.

He runs his fingers over the outside of my arm, around my collarbone and down my left breast, pausing briefly to admire my nipple.

I take a deep sigh and let it out.

"What are you afraid of Ellie?" Mr. Black whispers.

I close my eyes.

"I'm afraid of everything. I'm afraid of making mistakes so I live my life without taking any chances. I want to be a writer, but I'm afraid that I'll fail so I spend my days writing quizzes instead of something that really interests me."

"And what interests you?" he asks, making his way down to my navel.

"Well, right now, sex."

"And what about writing about sex?" he asks, teasing me.

"I've never thought about it before. But it seems like a scary thing to do. I mean, what if people I knew read my books?"

"And what if writing about this fulfilled your every desire and quenched every fear? What if it made you a writer? Would you take that chance?"

I nod without opening my eyes.

"Tell me how you would've wanted to lose your virginity, Ellie," Mr. Black says.

"What do you mean?" I open my eyes.

"The real stories of how we lost our virginities are often fraught with conflict and are quite sad. At least, that's my experience. So, I want you to tell me how you would've wanted to lose your virginity if you could do it again. Tell me your fantasy, Ellie."

I close my eyes and try to think about what he had just asked of me. I've never really given it much thought. But my thoughts return to what happened on the yacht today. This has been one of the most erotic and sensual experiences of my life. What would it be like to lose my virginity here?

"I guess it would have to be at an auction," I say slowly.

"An auction? Really?" He is genuinely surprised by the concept.

"Yeah. Actually, it was really sexy not knowing who was going to buy me, so to speak. It helped that most of the men on the boat were quite sexy, though," I say, laughing.

"But what about the old dudes?"

"Okay, maybe in this make believe virgin auction only hot guys are allowed to participate."

"Yes, of course. Hot guys with lots of money," he says. "Okay, keep going. I want to hear more about your fantasy."

"Well, I'm standing at the auction and the auctioneer makes me take off my clothes. I have to remove every last stitch."

"Mmm-mmm," Mr. Black licks his lips.

"And the auction goes high. There's a bidding frenzy. Because all the men want me."

"I can see that. Does it go up to a quarter million?"

"Yes, actually, higher than that. Remember, I am a virgin," I say.

"Wow, now that's hot. Going where no man has ever gone before."

"And then a tall, dark, handsome man in the back gets the winning bid. Once they transfer the money to my account, he leads me away to his room and does bad things to me."

"Bad things like what?"

"Actually, nothing like what we've done of course. I mean, I am a virgin. But he really pleasures me. And I pleasure him."

"I like the sound of that," he says. Suddenly, he leans over and kisses me. His lips are soft and persistent and they force mine open. When our tongues touch, a warm sensation spreads through my whole body.

He climbs on top of me. He wraps my head with his large hands and cradles it with his strong powerful body. When he starts to grind on me, I feel that large bulge that I've already felt, but have not yet seen.

"Slow down," I whisper. He looks up, briefly pulling away from my mouth.

"I want to watch you undress," I say.

I feel the power dynamic between us shifting. I'm no longer his servant and now I'm the one who is making demands. He flashes me a smile, with a twinkle in his eye.

"Okay, then," he says and gets off the bed.

He stands with his legs slightly apart and begins to take off his clothes. First he removes his tie and throws it over me. Jokingly, I put the loop over my head and drop it in between my breasts.

"Mmmm, that's a delicious look."

"Okay, okay, keep going," I say.

Next, Mr. Black removes his jacket and slowly unbuttons his starched, white shirt. Once it's unbuttoned, I finally get a glimpse of that rock hard body that I've been feeling through his clothes. When he removes the shirt, I admire the outline of every muscle and indentation. His skin is tan and smooth without a single hair. His stomach is a perfect six pack even when he's just standing there, relaxing before me. His shoulder muscles bulge out giving his broad shoulders a wide and rounded look, making me even wetter than I was already.

I watch as his hands move to his pants and he slowly unbuckles the belt and the top button. It pops open with ease and the zipper quickly follows. Suddenly, the pants drop to the floor, exposing his strong powerful thigh muscles.

"Someone didn't skip leg day at the gym," I joke.

"Hell no," he shakes his head.

Once he steps out of his pants and removes his socks, all that's left is tight, short, briefs. They're black and fit him like a glove, perfectly accentuating the large hard-on that's bursting out from underneath.

"You like?" Mr. Black asks.

I nod my head and lick my lips. When he tenses his stomach muscles to pull off his briefs, a defined V forms on the outside of them, pointing straight at his cock. I inhale deeply, unable to believe that I'm about to have all of this inside of me.

His body is so perfect that I have to pinch myself just to convince myself that this isn't a dream and that I didn't accidentally die and go to heaven.

"Are you drooling?" he asks, pulling off his briefs.

I wipe my mouth and realize that yes, I actually am.

"Well, it's not every day that a girl sees something like this."

I have to physically force myself to look away from his body and to his face. But as soon as he stands back up, I know that there's no way I will be able to. There's a large, gorgeous, erect cock staring back at me.

"Kiss me," he whispers.

"I thought you'd never ask," I say and grab his cock and wrap my lips around him.

"Oh wow, that's not what I meant...but okay..." he says, moaning in pleasure.

I'm not a girl who really enjoys blow jobs, not at all. In fact, most of the time, the thought doesn't even really occur to me unless the guy asks. But Mr. Black is different. After everything he's done to me tonight, after all the teasing and the flirting, I just had to have it. I love the way he fills up my mouth and I get wet thinking about what it would be like to have him inside of me. I want to have him like I never wanted to have anyone. No, it's more than want. I *need* to have him.

He puts his hands around my head and moves his body faster and faster in and out of my mouth. When I look up at him, I see that he has his head tilted back and his eyes closed from pleasure. But then suddenly, he slows down and pulls out of me.

"Kiss me," he says, lifting my chin up. I pull myself up on my knees, so that we're almost at eye level. His voice sounds so desperate and raw and needy that it sends shivers through my body.

I press my lips to his. His bottom lip is a little bit fuller than his top and my lips collide softly with his. We fall into a natural rhythm. First, he tilts my head to one side. And then another. Somehow, breaths manage to make it in between us. Our tongues intertwine and become one.

I pull away a little, but then he pulls me closer. He puts his right hand around my jaw and slowly makes his way toward the back of my neck and head. His fingers dig into my hair and pull slightly. The sensation feels so good, I nearly lose control. His lips pull stronger on me. They are trying to devour me. Taste every last bit of me. I bathe in the softness of the warm draft of air that escapes his lips in between our kisses.

Quietly, I start to moan. I am losing all control, beginning with the sounds that are escaping from my mouth. His body presses closer to me. I feel the thickness of his beautiful cock on my pelvic bone and my legs open up by themselves. His dick starts to nudge me in between my thighs, not really going all the way in, just teasing me. Just then he pulls away for a second and slips on a condom. It's a good thing one of us is being safe because I'm so lost in his body and in the moment that the thought of safe sex didn't even occur to me.

A few seconds later, he's back in front of me. Pushing into my body with his. Teasing me with his kisses. Suddenly, my legs give out and we collapse onto the bed. Even though I feel like I can't handle anymore, I want more. I need more of him. Finally, he pushes himself inside of me and I scream out in pleasure. He is taking me and giving me everything that I never knew I needed or wanted. I never felt pleasure like this. It's like every molecule in my body is suddenly excited and dancing.

He continues to thrust in and out of me and I continue to moan with each thrust. I feel like I'm on the verge of orgasm, but I don't want to get there just yet. I need this to last. I want to stay in this moment forever. Suddenly, and without pulling out of me, he bows his head and places my breast into his mouth.

"You have the most perfect breasts, Ellie," he whispers. "I want to have them in my mouth always."

He bites down on my nipple slightly, sending a shooting sensation of pleasure mixed with pain through my whole body. Whatever little space existed between us becomes filled with pleasure. I close my eyes and allow myself to feel everything, every last delicious bit of his body, and this moment that we're sharing.

"Oh my God," I moan. He groans on top of me, pushing himself even further within me. Suddenly, I lose all control. I fall into euphoria and start to see stars, both with my eyes open and closed. My hips buck into him and the warmest sensation releases over my entire body. But this time, it's not just warm. It's hot. I actually have something of a hot flash as my body starts to convulse underneath him. I want him more than I ever wanted anything in my whole life. The thought of him pulling out of me in this moment is enough to make me weep. Big round tears roll down my cheeks without my permission. They just appear from the pleasure of the orgasm.

"Wow," he whispers in my ear, as he continues to thrust into me but much slower and gentler this time. "How was that?"

I wipe my tears and stretch out my toes. I can't feel my legs and I can barely even feel him anymore.

"Earth-shattering," I whisper.

"I kind of figured that," he smiles.

He continues to thrust within me. His movements are getting faster and faster. His bites become more hurried and his kisses become sloppier. He is losing control. I look into his eyes and watch it happen. He tilts his head back in pleasure. He also pulls away from my face, exposing his chiseled torso. As he pulls in and out of me, I watch as each muscle tenses and relaxes over and over. I feel a tingling come over my body again. I'm starting to get excited again. How many of these can I even have in one night?

"Ellie," he whispers and pushes in and out of me faster and faster. His breathing speeds up and then he finally reaches the climax. Every muscle in his body tenses including his face before a big relief sweeps over him. He gives me a few more small thrusts, before collapsing on top of me, covered in sweat.

"Oh my God, Ellie," he says, trying to catch his breath. "That was amazing."

"Yes, it was," I nod.

The room is silent while we both think about what we've just done. The experience was something beyond what I ever experienced before, or thought I would ever experience.

"It felt like we were dancing, didn't it? Like we were totally in sync?" he asks.

I nod. "It felt like we were one."

He nods and rolls over on his back, then pulls off the condom with one swift motion. Drops of sweat glisten on his six pack and it takes all of my willpower not to lean over and lick them off him.

I run my finger up and down his washboard abs, pausing over each grove.

"Your body is...unreal," I say. He smiles.

"I have seven percent body fat," he boasts.

"Wow. That must take a lot of effort."

"It did at first," he says. "But now, it's just my life. I love working out. I actually feel sick if I skip a day or two."

"So, what we just did? Does that count as exercise?" I ask, coyly.

"Actually, given the amount that I'm sweating, I'd say yes."

We lay there staring into space for some time. It takes a few minutes of staring into space and trying to collect my thoughts about what just happened to realize just how comfortable the bed really is. The sheets are so luxurious, they are probably 1000-thread count. The pillows are just fluffy enough without losing their shape, molding perfectly to my head. I close my eyes to savor the moment.

———

SOMETIME LATER, I wake up. I'm not sure how much time has passed, but Mr. Black is not in the bed next to me. I stretch, marvel at the comfort of the sheets again and then finally pull myself out of bed. When I walk over to the windows and pull on the curtains, I see that the sun is high in the sky. It's daylight.

Last night, seems like nothing but a dream. Did it really happen? Did all that really take place? Frankly, I have a hard time believing that Mr. Black is even real. Do people like him even exist? So, kind and caring and demanding at the same time. Someone who is both a mystery and an open book?

I look around the suite and after confirming that he is not there, I leave and make my way toward my own room. There, I jump into the shower and wash off all the sweat and sex from my body. On one hand, the shower is refreshing, but on the other, it makes me feel sad. I love the smell of Mr. Black on my hands and body and now a little part of him is gone.

After putting on some eyeliner and mascara and darkening my brows a little bit, I hear a knock at the door. It's Lizbeth.

"I'm just here to check on you. How was everything last night?" she asks.

"Great," I say. "Actually it was really great."

"Well, I'm glad to hear that," she says smiling from ear to ear.

"And everything is alright with your account?" she asks.

"Um, I don't actually know. That's a good question."

"Well, I can wait while you double check, it's no problem."

That wasn't exactly what I had in mind, but okay. I pull out my phone and log into my Bank of America account. I have exactly $251,459.39 in there. The quarter million is from last night and the $1,459 and some change is what I previously had to live on for the rest of the month. Wow, it didn't seem like such a paltry amount until just now.

"Yes, everything seems to be in order."

"I'm glad to hear that. Well, in any case, I just want to let you know that there's breakfast in the dining room. And the helicopter is ready to take you back to Manhattan at any time."

Oh. Wait, what? A helicopter? I'm stunned for a moment.

"Do I have to go back right now?" I ask.

"No, of course not, you can definitely have breakfast first, if you like."

"No, that's not exactly what I meant," I say hesitantly. "What I mean is that I thought that this was going to be a weekend thing. I thought there was maybe another party later on?"

Lizbeth flashes a mysterious smile at me.

"Oh, so you really had a good time last night,"

she says. My cheeks turn bright red and then I blush even more from the thought that I'm embarrassed.

"Mr. Black does leave an impression, doesn't he?" Lizbeth asks.

From the tone of her voice, I can tell that she's probably not a stranger in his bed. The thought of that makes me really mad, but I try to keep a hold of my temper.

"Never-mind. I guess I was misinformed," I mumble and turn back to my suitcase and pretend to pack.

"Listen, the party was just for one night. I mean the party continues, but there will be another auction tonight. With all new girls. The men here like fresh meat so to say."

"Yes, of course. I'm such an idiot."

"No, you're not," Lizbeth says, putting her arm around my shoulder. "You just didn't know."

There's a real tenderness in this moment. I suddenly feel like she knows exactly how I feel. The disappointment and the regret mixed with anger and jealousy. I want to know more about her.

"So, how did you get this job?" I ask her.

"I came here just like you, a few years go. Someone bought me and we had a very good time. Then he asked me to stay for a week. And then a

month. And then I started to serve him all
the time."

"What do you mean?" I ask.

"Well, we have what you would call a master-
slave relationship. I am here to serve him and do
anything he wants. Indefinitely."

"And you like that?"

"Oh yes," she nods her head. "I have never felt
anything this exhilarating in my entire life. It helps
that we are very sexually compatible."

"So, who is he? Your master?" I ask. The word
feels uncomfortable in my mouth and I cringe a
little when it comes out. But there's also something
exciting about the thought.

"He's a friend of Mr. Black's. He's away now on
business, that's why I'm here entertaining you all on
Mr. Black's yacht. Otherwise, I'd be on his yacht."

"What's his name?" I ask.

"Mr. White."

I laugh out loud. "Do they all have names
like that?"

"Yes, they do," she nods her head. "They are part
of a loose organization called The Billionaire Boys
Club. The members are the ones who own the
yachts. The other men who were in the hall bidding
are prospective members."

"Wow, I had no idea," I whisper.

"It's somewhat of a secret organization. They don't like to talk about it very openly because many run very large, multinational companies with shareholders. Lots of people to answer to."

"So, how long have you been with Mr. White?" I ask. "And are you two together?"

"Yes, actually. We have been exclusive for more than two years now. He even asked me to marry him."

"Oh wow, congratulations," I say.

She smiles. "It's definitely not what my parents from Kentucky had in mind, but I love him. Very much."

With that, Lizbeth bids me farewell. Before she leaves she does tell me that if Mr. Black wants to contact me again, he will. Otherwise, I will probably never see him again.

I decide to forgo breakfast and head straight to the helicopter. If I'm not invited to stay here any longer then that's fine by me. I have my quarter of a million dollars and quite a memory.

When I get to the helicopter pad, I see that I'm the only one there. The pilot waves me over. Rolling my suitcase behind me, I walk over to the helicopter. The pilot asks me for my address and says that he'll land on top of a building only a few blocks away. He helps me with my luggage and hands me a headset to wear. I climb into the backseat.

Someone comes over the radio and tells him to wait. I figure that there're more girls going back, so I sit back in my chair and look out at the deep blue ocean spreading all the way to the horizon.

"Hey there," a familiar deep voice says. When I turn around, I see that it's none other than Mr. Black.

Shivers run down my spine and a big wide smile comes over my face.

"You didn't think you'd get rid of me so soon," he says and helps me out of the helicopter.

"What are you doing here?" I ask.

"Just wanted to say good-bye. After the night we had, we need a proper good-bye, don't you think?"

I nod and press my lips to his. I wrap my arms around his strong muscular shoulders and let him hold me up as he kisses me back.

"I'm sorry. I'd ask you stay another night, but I have a work thing back in New York," Mr. Black says after he finally pulls away.

"That's okay, I understand."

"So, I just wanted to wish you a good flight and tell you that I want to see you again. Soon."

A big smile comes over my face. I actually feel my eyes twinkle from happiness. I know that it's probably not a good idea, but there's something that's drawing me to him. I have to be with him. Need to be with him on some sub-atomic level.

"I'd like that," I say coyly trying not to sound too eager.

"Good," he says. "Here's my card. It has my private cell number on it."

I look at the elegant white business card on thick, expensive paper. It may be a business card, but it's not the one he uses for work. The name on the card reads Mr. Black.

"Do you need mine?" I ask.

"Actually, Lizbeth already gave it to me. She had it on the paperwork you filled out for the auction."

I don't know what to say, so I kiss him again. He reciprocates in kind.

"By the way, my name is Aiden," he whispers into my ear after he pulls away. "Aiden Black."

I climb back into the helicopter as if I'm floating on a cloud. Before closing the door, he kisses me on the hand and wishes me a good flight.

I keep my eyes on Aiden as we fly away and I keep looking long after he and the yacht disappear into the ocean.

When the New York skyline appears before us on the horizon, my phone beeps and I look down at the text.

"Now, you have the full $250,000 to be unwise with. Go live your life to the fullest. Pursue your dreams. Nothing else in the world is worth it."

The number is a perfect match to the one on the card that Aiden gave me. It takes me a minute to realize what he means by the full $250,000. But I still don't believe it until I can see it with my own eyes. Quickly, I log into my student loan account. And instead of $151,329, which I owed last month, the balance now reads $0.00.

"You paid off my student loans??" I text Aiden.

"Yes."

"Why?"

"Because you deserve the full quarter million to be unwise with."

I shake my head, not believing that any of this is really real. Who the hell are you Aiden Black?

CHAPTER 16 - MR. BLACK

I'm not a big fan of the opera.

Well, that's an understatement. I actually hate it.

Everything about it is so pretentious and exhausting.

The music is over the top and so are the actors' mannerisms and gestures.

Some people love this place so much that they cry because they are so moved by the music.

Well, I don't.

In fact, I wish that I could put in my ear buds and listen to something I do actually like.

Like the Stones.

Or Led Zeppelin.

I love classic rock.

Now, if they actually made a rock opera...then that's something I'd watch.

So, why am I here?

I definitely don't need to be here in my line of work.

Even though everyone in tech is really rich, we aren't money rich.

So, you'd be hard-pressed enough to find any of us wearing a suit and tie, let alone going to the symphony or the opera.

Unlike the rest of them, who spend their days in t-shirts and jeans, I love a nice tailored suit that costs double what my childhood home's mortgage was.

But the opera?

I'm definitely not a fan.

No, the only reason I'm here is that Kristina insisted that we come.

Kristina Taylor is a class act.

I've known her for a very long time.

We met at some Ivy League mixer back in college when I was at Yale and she was at Brown.

Kristina and I never dated.

Our sexual appetites and desires are way too similar.

Kristina doesn't believe in relationships and I

don't either, that is if you don't count that brief lapse in judgement when I got married.

I glance over at Kristina, who is wholeheartedly engrossed in The Metropolitan Opera's critically acclaimed production of George Bizet's *Carmen*.

The tickets to this show were not only ridiculously expensive but they were also impossible to get and it's all because of the French mezzo-soprano Clementine Margaine who stars as the immortal Gypsy heroine.

"I saw Maria Agresta in her debut last year in La Boheme last season," Kristina whispers, wiping a tear away after a particularly touching performance.

"Yeah, she's great," I say without much enthusiasm.

Kristina returns her gaze to the stage and I return mine to her.

Her pale white skin and her long, thin fingers make her look delicate, but I know quite well what they are capable of and it's not at all delicate.

You see, Kristina is one of the most popular and well-paid dominatrix in New York City, which pretty much makes her one of the top dominatrixes in the world.

You'd never guess it from the outside.

No, from the outside, she still looks like a shy

librarian and the lost little English major that I remember back in college.

But then again, as you probably already know, you should never judge a book by its cover.

"Quit staring at me," she whispers, without taking her eyes off the stage.

"I'm just imagining all the bad things I'm going to do to you tonight," I whisper back.

She shakes her head, but a small coy smile forms at the edge of her lips, which tells me that she's looking forward to it, too.

As far as I know, Kristina and I have a unique relationship.

What I mean is that while I continue to play with other women on the side, Kristina doesn't.

Kristina is a dominant for a living, but she likes to be the submissive when we are together.

She likes being tied up and she enjoys all the little dirty things that I do to her to make her orgasm over and over.

"If you keep this up, I'm not coming over," she says defiantly.

She might be bluffing, but I can't tell for sure. So, I decide to play it safe.

———

WHEN WE ARRIVE BACK at my place, I'm dying of anticipation.

My mind has been running in circles, all throughout the performance, of all the bad things that we're going to do together, and my dick has been rock hard since the intermission.

"Hey, baby." I press her against the kitchen counter and kiss her neck.

She throws her head back and moans a little. "I have some nice things planned for you."

"I can't wait."

Before heading into my special room, I glance one last time at her dress.

Luckily, it's a little black strapless number, which I can slide all the way down. Good. This means that her arms can be otherwise occupied.

Kristina walks confidently into the room and looks around.

She has been here a number of times before.

She's even used it for her own clients on a few occasions.

They were very exclusive clients, and she owed me big afterward as I don't allow just anyone to play around in here.

She glances up at the swing hanging from the ceiling and winks at me.

I know what she wants.

She wants me to tie her hands up there and lift her up.

She loves that.

Being weightless.

Hanging in space while I make her orgasm over and over again.

"Oh, sir, please be careful with me," she says flirtatiously.

Being called sir is the lingo which sets up the power dynamic between us.

It's as much of a turn-on for her as it is for me.

"We'll see about that," I say and put her hands into the restraints above her head.

I unzip her dress and pull it down to her feet.

She steps out of it.

I notice that she's not wearing either underwear or a bra.

"Wow, I wasn't prepared for that," I say.

My cock gets so hard it feels like it turned into a rock.

I spread her legs wide and tie them with rope so that they stay apart after I start.

I look at her and lick my lips.

She tries to put a frightened expression on her face, but she isn't very successful.

Instead, she looks like it's taking all of her energy to keep her excitement and anticipation at bay.

And then suddenly, last weekend pops into my head.

And not just last weekend, but Ellie to be precise.

Her soft lips, her luscious breasts.

Her defying me and orgasming without my permission.

I try to snap out of it and turn my attention to Kristina, but my mind refuses to cooperate.

All I can see is Ellie here. All I want is Ellie.

"What's taking so long?" Kristina asks. "Are you going to start or what?"

I look at her.

Her pale skin is a shade or two too light in comparison to Ellie's.

Her eyes aren't the right shape.

Even her body is suddenly a little too thin.

No, the problem is not that there's anything wrong with Kristina.

It's just that she's not Ellie.

"I'm sorry. I can't do this," I say and untie her leg restraints.

When I bring the swing down to the floor and undo her arm restraints, she slaps me across the face.

"What do you mean you can't do this?" Kristina asks. "Who the hell do you think you are?"

"I'm sorry, but my head is just not in this tonight."

"Well, get in this."

She goes to slap me again, but I catch her hand before it reaches my face.

"Please, don't do that again. Ever," I whisper in my most dead-serious voice.

"You're an asshole, you know that!" Kristina yells, grabbing her dress and shoes, walking out of the room.

CHAPTER 17 - ELLIE

WHEN I SEE MY BEST FRIEND AGAIN...

I love New York in the fall.

It has only been a few days since I got back from the yacht, but fall seems to have descended on New York with a vengeance.

The streets are wet and slick, and trees are already changing colors.

When I open the window to my room, I fall in love with that smell of fresh rain on the cool asphalt.

The large oak tree in front of our apartment is already turning shades of gold.

There is something about this time of year that makes me want to buy stationary supplies even though I don't go to school anymore.

Perhaps I may indulge myself, nevertheless, and get a new writer's notebook and some pens.

Without getting out of bed, I stretch out and yawn, curling my toes.

Suddenly, I have a flashback to the toe-curling orgasms that Mr. Black gave me only a few days ago.

I don't know if I will see him again, but I know that I will not forget that night with him for a very, very long time.

Climbing out of bed, my body shivers, remembering the pleasure that he had given me.

As someone who isn't afraid to identify myself as a feminist, because I firmly believe that men and women deserve the same pay for the same work and equal rights, I was definitely not the most obvious candidate for the type of auction that I participated in on that luxurious yacht last weekend.

If someone had brought it up to me before, I would've dismissed them without giving them a second thought.

But when the time came, it seemed like an exciting and fun thing to do.

Exciting because I didn't know what to expect or who I would get. But never in my wildest dreams did I think that I would get anyone like Mr. Black.

"Hey, bitch!" Caroline bursts into my room. It's only six in the morning and we both have to work, but she just got home.

"Another fun night out?" I ask, pointing to her short evening dress and heels that are much more appropriate for the club than for that high-end art gallery in Soho where she works.

"Actually, I met this really hot guy.

He works on Wall Street," she says, unzipping her dress and motioning for me to follow her to the other room.

"Is that the type of guy that you always meet?" I ask.

"I don't know what to say; the exclusive clubs around here are littered with them," she says, shrugging. "But he was really cute. And really good in bed. He was wasted, so I can just imagine how good he'd be if he didn't drink so much."

I nod and head to the bathroom to brush my teeth.

"He wanted me to sleep over, actually," she yells from the other room.

"Wow, that is different," I mumble through the toothpaste in my mouth.

"I know, right?" Caroline pops in the doorway. "I wasn't going to, but then, get this? I just fell asleep. How embarrassing, right?"

I shrug. It doesn't sound that embarrassing actually.

"Oh, c'mon. I don't want him to think I'm some loser who's going to be a hanger on. I really like this guy. And guys like a challenge."

Caroline is very experienced with men, but all of her experience just seems to have manifested itself into a broad theoretical interpretation of how you shouldn't act around men.

You'd think that there would be a purpose to theories - like if she was on the lookout for the right one, the marrying kind.

But, no, Caroline isn't interested in that at all. She thinks of dating as one elaborate game and one that she has to win at all costs.

Caroline disappears into her room for a few moments, giving me just enough time to wash my face and put dry shampoo in my hair.

I usually shower at night because I can't stand lukewarm showers, and hot showers leave my face with red splotchy spots that refuse to go away.

Unfortunately, most of the time, my hair gets greasy just from sleeping on it and requires a strict dry shampoo regimen even the following day.

"Oh my God!" Caroline shrieks at the top of her lungs, nearly giving me a heart attack. "I almost forgot!"

I stare at her with my hair pulled back in a loose

ponytail and my hand in desperate search of a
hair tie.

Where the hell do they always go? I just bought a
pack of them at Rite Aid last week and now nearly
half of them are already gone!

"You have to tell me what happened on the
yacht! And the auction!" Caroline jumps up
and down.

A part of me thought that she would be so
engrossed in the aftermath of her own date that she
would completely forget about my weekend.

But, apparently, I had no such luck.

"It was fun actually," I say. "Really fun."

"Okay, you're not getting off that easy."

"Okay, but only if you pay for breakfast." I finally
cave. She gives out another shriek and
wholeheartedly agrees.

We go to the local cafe for an avocado omelet
and brioche toast.

Even though she's tall and lean and built like a
model, Caroline is again on a diet, avoiding all carbs
as if they are poison.

Despite my much curvier body, which is still
carrying around ten or fifteen pounds more than I
want, I enjoy my toast immensely. When the waiter
comes back with a second cup of tea for me and a

third cup of coffee for Caroline, I finally finish my story.

At first, when I agreed to tell her everything, I thought that I would leave out all the really dirty bits of what happened.

But as I started talking and really got into reliving what happened that weekend, I didn't want to.

I wanted to capture it just as it happened.

And if I can't share this story with Caroline, my closest friend, then who the hell can I tell this to?

"So, you got $250,000 for just spending one night with him?" she asks.

"Well, actually more. I must've made an impression because he paid off my school loans of $150,000, so now I have the full quarter million to do with whatever."

"Holy shit." She shakes her head.

She actually looks impressed. Caroline's family may own half of New England, but this amount is a lot even for her.

"Having regrets?" I ask.

"Actually, yes." She nods. "I honestly thought that they'd maybe go up to ten or fifteen thousand, but not a quarter of a million."

"Well, most girls got around a hundred

thousand." I point out. "Which is still really fucking good."

"Fuck me." She shakes her head.

Her family may have a lot of money, but like all kids who are raised in wealth, she knows very well that that money comes with certain restrictions.

She's only entitled to it if she follows the rules.

The rules aren't too strict, but they're still rules.

"The thing is that beyond the money, I just had a really wonderful time. Mr. Black...was amazing. He was unlike anyone else I've ever met. He was just so...arousing."

"Wow, smitten-kitten much?"

"I know. I must sound like a love-sick teenager," I say.

"So, you think you'll see him again?" Caroline asks.

Now, there's a loaded question. I inhale and exhale deeply before answering.

"I didn't at first. I mean, it's only just supposed to be a one-night thing. But he gave me his card and took my number."

"Oh my God, really?"

"I still don't know if he'll call," I say.

"If he gave you his card, you can always call him," Caroline says.

Of course, that's true.

I just don't know if I can actually do that.

I'm not Caroline.

Actually, I've never called a guy and asked him out for a date before.

And I'm definitely not going to start with Mr. Black of all people.

I glance at the time. Shit, I'm going to be late.

"I have to go," I mutter and get my purse.

"And why is it again that you're going to that shitty job of yours?" Caroline asks, signing the check.

I don't have a good reason except that it's work.

"You do realize that you are a very rich woman now?"

I nod and give her a peck on the cheek. "I have to go. I'll see you tonight."

Fifteen minutes later, I arrive at the office drenched in sweat.

Even though it's fall, it's still rather warm and humid outside and running all those blocks to the office does not leave me in the most presentable shape.

When I enter the office, the first person I lay my eyes on is Tom, one of my closest friends and my secret crush of more two years.

His desk is only a few away from mine, usually giving me an optimal spot for watching the way his gorgeous hair falls into his face as he works.

Tom waves at me excitedly and I wave back, but the butterflies in the pit of my stomach that I usually feel every time I am in his presence are gone.

Completely. I don't quite believe it.

I walk over to my desk and drop my bag to the floor.

"You're late," Tom says, coming over to my desk. "She was expecting you fifteen minutes ago."

"Late for what?" I ask.

He stares at me as if I have completely lost my mind.

"Carrie? You have a meeting with her this morning?"

Oh, shit.

Suddenly, I remember.

Carrie Warrenhouse, the beautiful and hard as nails editor of BuzzPost and Tom's fiancée, wanted to see me first thing Monday morning.

Oh, shit.

Shit.

Shit.

"You forgot?" Tom asks. "I can't believe you forgot."

Well, I can't believe that you are marrying that bitch, I want to say, but I keep my mouth shut.

Instead, I look through my very disorganized bag for a notepad and a pen so that I have something to write with in case she has any notes for me.

When I first started here, I learned the hard way that Carrie always has notes and finds it insulting if you don't come to her office prepared.

"Here, here," Tom says, grabbing a notepad from his desk. "Do you at least have a pen?"

I find a pen on my desk and display it for him proudly.

"Thank you," I say and head toward her office.

WHEN THINGS AT WORK DON'T GO AS PLANNED...

*C*arrie Warrenhouse.

She's the current editor of BuzzPost and the daughter of the Edward Warrenhouse, the current owner of BuzzPost.

It would be one thing if she was a total incompetent idiot, but the thing is that she's not.

Not at all.

She's smart and incredibly put together.

Despite her rich family, she probably would've gotten into Harvard all on her own accord.

She's five years older than Tom and I are and, over the last few years, she's made BuzzPost an actual contender in the game of serious news.

It made its mark on the world with wacky videos and funny online quizzes, but over the last few years that she has been Editor in Chief, they really transitioned into reporting on important political and international news.

And, unlike other online magazines and newspapers, they continue to make money off it.

Advertisers love us and the money is pouring in.

"Please have a seat, Ellie," Carrie says, pointing to the plush chair in front of her desk.

Her office has floor-to-ceiling windows and a beautiful view of the skyline.

"I'm sorry I'm late," I mumble and crouch down into the seat.

I don't know what we're going to talk about, but meetings like this always make me nervous.

I feel like I've been called to the principal's office and she's about to call my mom and report me.

Carrie is the epitome of chic.

Her hair is styled in a short razor-sharp bob without a single strand out of place.

In comparison, my own long unkempt tresses, which kindly may be described as styled as beach waves, look unprofessional and out of control.

I twirl a lock around my index finger, regretting the fact that I didn't even bother running a brush through them this morning.

"I wanted to discuss with you the last article that you submitted," she says.

This place has about ten editors, but Carrie is such a micro-manager and workaholic that she oversees every part of the BuzzPost with utmost precision.

"Uh-huh." I nod.

For the life of me, I can't even remember what the article was about.

"It's this one, about the Kardashians and their new makeup line," she says.

Oh, yes, of course.

Now, that's some hard-hitting journalism right there.

"From reading it, I got the sense that you were not particularly interested in the topic," she says, pointing to the printed out article on her desk.

I glance over and see that it's all marked up in red. Shit.

"Well, you know, it's kind of a fluff piece."

Double shit. I should not have said that.

"A fluff piece?" Carrie asks with a look of shock and contempt on her face. "Are you serious?"

"No, what I mean is that." I try to backtrack, but nothing really comes to mind. "I didn't really mean that."

"I'll wait," Carrie says, crossing her arms across her chest.

What a bitch. It takes all of my power to keep myself from rolling my eyes.

"It's just a sponsored post about their new makeup line," I say.

"Exactly. It's a sponsored post, and that means that we're getting paid good money for publishing it. And that's why a story like this needs a writer who can at least fake a minimal amount of excitement about the products and the Kardashian brand in general."

Are you serious?

I want to scream.

Are you fucking serious?

I mean, we both went to Ivy League schools and now you're asking me to show more excitement for the Kardashians?

It's not that I have anything against them.

It's just that I don't actually really know anything, or really care to know anything, about them.

But, of course, I can't express any of this. Instead, I bite my tongue and say, "I understand."

"The thing is Ellie, that this is not just a one off problem with you," Carrie says. "This is becoming something of a habit. I have been reviewing some of your other work and, frankly, I think you can do a lot better."

I nod as if I agree with her.

There's nothing really to say since they did publish my other articles.

"I know that your direct editor seems to be happy, but I expect more. I want BuzzPost to be one of the top online magazines around, and we're not going to get there if our writers are not on top of their game."

"Okay, I'll try," I mumble.

But Carrie doesn't let it go. She just keeps pushing.

"I don't need you to just try, Ellie. I need you to do."

Finally, I've had enough.

"I don't really know what you want me to say," I say after a moment of silence. "I mean, I'm sorry if you think my work isn't up to some standard, but I think it's pretty good. Frankly, I think I got as excited about the Kardashian makeup line as any sane person could get. But if you want to employ a celebrity-obsessed teenager to write these kind of articles, be my guest."

Oh my God.

I can't believe I just said that.

I'm not an outgoing person, and I've never said what I really thought to a boss before.

From the look on Carrie's face, she seems to be a little bit caught off guard as well.

She straightens her tailored suit jacket and adjusts herself in her seat.

Suddenly, a strand of hair breaks off from the rest of her perfect bob, and she no longer seems so intimidating.

"I don't really know what to say to that, Ellie," she says after a moment. "Except that you don't really seem very happy here."

"Actually, I'm not. Not at all. I don't like writing the kind of fluff articles that I get assigned, and I don't really like to write articles that pretend to be journalism but are actually elaborate advertisements. That's not why I came here."

"Then maybe this place isn't the one for you."

I think about that for a moment.

She's right.

For the first time, I actually agree with her.

"No, it's not," I say, getting up. "Consider this my two weeks notice."

Before I get all the way to the other side of her office, she calls out, "Actually, we don't need two weeks notice. We can get the interns to fill in for you."

Wow, really?

I've worked here for almost two years and she's going to get the interns to do my work.

And she doesn't have to pay them anything.

Perfect.

I don't even bother to acknowledge her statement.

Instead, I walk out of her office and head straight to my desk.

CHAPTER 19 - ELLIE

WHEN MY SECRET CRUSH DISAPPEARS...

"Where are you going?" Tom comes over right away after my meeting.

I take my bag and start to put personal things from my desk into it.

"What are you doing? What's going on, Ellie?"

I shrug.

I don't want to get into this now in front of everyone.

But I know Tom, he isn't the type to take a hint or to let something go.

"I just quit," I say.

Actually, given what happened, I'm not entirely sure how accurate that is.

I mean, I was going to quit in two weeks, but Carrie said I should go right away.

Does that even count like a quit? Or did I just get fired?

I can't keep track of all the thoughts that are running through my head anymore.

And I definitely don't have any answers to any of it.

"What? Why?" Tom gasps.

I shrug.

"It was a long time coming," I say after a moment. "I mean, I can't really write long advertisements disguised as articles anymore. Or stupid quizzes."

Tom knows exactly what I'm talking about.

He was a political science major at Yale.

He's a political junkie and, despite the fact that he's really qualified and engaged to the editor, he still spends most of his days coming up with quizzes like, "*Design a dream apartment and we'll tell you who you are* and *This Ben & Jerry's Quiz will tell you which Hogwarts House you belong in*."

After stuffing my purse with almost everything that I brought into the office, I wave good-bye to some of my other colleagues and walk out to the elevators.

I'm not friends with anyone here except for Tom,

and we all live nearby so it's not like I'm not going to run into them again. Tom follows me.

"Ellie, what's going on?" Tom asks, grabbing my shoulder.

I shrug him off.

"Nothing. It's just something I've been thinking about for a while. I mean, this place is fine, but I just can't work here anymore."

"This is one of the top places to work in New York if you want to be a writer," Tom says. "I mean, I know that Carrie can be a real bitch sometimes. What did she say?"

Did he really just say that about his fiancée? I shake my head.

"It's not her. It's everything. I want to write what I want to write, Tom. And I'm sick of being here. My mind is made up."

We ride down the elevator together in silence.

"But what about money? Do you really want to depend on Mitch for everything again?" he asks.

"Wow, really, Tom? You're going to bring that up?"

We've been friends for a long time.

And, as a result, he is very well familiar with my issues with my stepfather.

I grew up in a very middle-class family that pretty much lived paycheck to paycheck. But after my parents divorced when I was eight, my mom took a job tutoring Mitch Willoughby's five-year-old daughter.

Mitch was a widower and a vice-president at one of the top investment banks in New York.

They fell in love and married soon after that and they have been happily together for many years now.

I don't really have any issues with Mitch except that he wants to do a little bit too much for me.

He wants to pay for everything and, sometimes, even takes offense when I want to pay for my own things.

One of the reasons why I really wanted to take this job after graduation was that I wanted to pay my own way, at least as far I could.

He still pays for my share of the apartment that I share with Caroline because there's no way I could afford it otherwise.

Given the fact that Tom's dad is also quite wealthy and he lives in a crappy fourth-floor walkup and refuses to take any money from him, I thought that unlike anyone else we know, he would really understand where I'm coming from.

"I just don't get what you're doing, Ellie.

Suddenly, when things get a little tough, you're just going to quit? You know you would never really be able to do that if it weren't for Mitch, right?"

It's hard to believe that his pride is one of the things that I actually admired about him before.

"Are you really going to make me feel guilty about this?"

"Yes! I mean, no. I don't want to make you feel guilty. I just want you to stay. I mean, you're like my only friend there."

"Aren't you forgetting someone?"

He stares at me.

"Carrie? The editor in chief? Your fiancée?"

"Yes, of course. But you know what I mean. She's from another world from us. You're the only one who really gets it."

Now, I feel insulted.

"The thing is Tom, that you're from a rich family. Your dad is a famous attorney at one of the most prestigious law firms in Boston. You summered on Cape Cod. You went to Yale. You're marrying into the Warrenhouse family, which owns half of New England. Mitch might have money, but my real father doesn't. He's a teacher. You may sympathize with the poor and live like you are poor, but it's not real."

"Fuck you, Ellie. I don't take any money from my dad. I live on what I make here. And thirty grand doesn't buy much in New York."

"No, it doesn't," I agree.

"And you don't think I don't want to quit this? You don't think I don't want to go on the campaign trail and follow and report on politics as it happens? Of course, I do. But I also want to pay my own way."

"Well, maybe you shouldn't," I say. "I mean, if your dad is willing to pay for you to start your political journalist career, why not let him? He loves you. You're not getting anywhere just working here, doing what you don't really want."

"I can't believe you're saying this to me," Tom says.

To be honest, I don't really believe it much either.

This was definitely not the opinion that I had even last week.

I admired what Tom was doing.

Living life on his own terms.

But now, with almost a quarter million dollars in my bank account, I feel a little different about money.

There's a freedom that comes with it.

The freedom to not do crap that you don't want to do.

Now, I don't have to waste my time writing pieces that I don't care about.

I can write what I want to write and really pursue my own dreams.

And getting the money wasn't all that bad either.

It was actually exciting.

Shivers run up my body as I think back to last weekend.

"Ellie? You're not listening to me," Tom says. He has been talking for a bit, but I have no idea what he said.

"Listen, what's done is done. I'm going to go home now. We can talk about this more if you want later," I say and walk away from him.

I don't know if it's the money or just meeting Mr. Black, but I no longer feel like a love-sick puppy around Tom.

Before last weekend, I'd spend my days waiting for him to come and talk to me at my desk.

I'd live for the moments of banter that we exchanged during lunch or on a coffee break.

I obsessed with his relationship with Carrie and their engagement.

But now, things are different. Tom is still a friend,

but the feelings that I had for him seemed to have all but dissipated.

It was like a balloon had popped and all the pressure that was built up inside had vanished.

When I get home, I don't even bother to unpack my bag, but just drop it to the floor. I sit down in front of my laptop and open a new document.

The story that I start isn't entirely fully-formed in my head, but I do have the beginning.

I don't know where it's headed, but for now I have the insatiable need to write down everything that happened.

It takes me a moment to decide where I want to start: with Caroline getting the invitation to the luxurious yacht party.

I type the title of the work at the top, *Auctioned to Him*, and begin.

With that, the words just start to spill out of me. My fingers can't type fast enough to keep up.

CHAPTER 20 - ELLIE

WHEN I HEAR HIS VOICE AGAIN...

I write for close to two hours without taking a break.

The words come and come like a waterfall. I've never had this experience before.

Suddenly, my phone rings.

I should've turned it off and go to do just that.

But when I glance at the screen I see that it's a call from him. Him.

Mr. Black.

And it's not just a phone call.

He's calling on FaceTime.

I don't have time to even glance at myself in the mirror, but I decide to answer it anyway.

"Hello, gorgeous," he says in his sultry, deep voice.

I almost forgot how sexy it was, but within a moment it all comes back to me.

He looks breathtaking.

His eyes are deep and wide with long, beautiful eyelashes.

His skin is tan and the way the light falls on it, he looks like he's almost glowing.

"Hey," I whisper.

Unfortunately, I glance at my own reflection in the lower right hand corner of the screen.

Unlike him, I do not present well.

The light here is coming from directly above me, giving me strange long shadows all over my face.

My nose looks to be double the size and don't even get me started on my bigger than usual forehead.

It's as if I didn't have it tough enough.

"I'm just calling to say hello," he says.

"It's really nice to hear from you," I say. And see you, but I don't add this.

"You seem surprised."

"Actually, I am." He isn't wrong about that.

"Why is that?"

"Well, you know." I shrug. "Men in New York. They promise to call, but never do. I'm kind of used to it."

I hate how defeated my voice sounds.

It sounds like I'm sitting around and waiting for them call me.

This is not the case.

Well, not in every case.

Agh, I am definitely not putting out a good impression.

"Ellie, you never met a man like me," he says confidently.

It takes me a moment to catch my breath.

Something within me sighs and surrenders, and my body relaxes with pleasure.

I crave his presence.

I need him to be here, next to me.

I need to press my body against his.

I shudder at the thought.

I've never felt like this before.

On the surface, the feeling seems like lust.

But I've felt lust before, and it never felt like this.

"What is it?" he asks.

Suddenly, I realize that I haven't said anything for quite some time.

"Nothing. You just caught me by surprise," I mumble.

I look at his face more closely.

It's breathtaking.

His dark hair is lustrous and thick, and imagining running my fingers through it makes me weak at the knees.

"So, the reason I'm calling is that I want to see you again, gorgeous."

The way he says gorgeous makes both of my cheeks turn bright red.

"Okay. Like on a date?"

"You could say that. Something of an extended date."

I don't really know what he means, so he explains.

"I want you to be mine for the week. Just like you were mine for a night. If you agree, you would have to do everything I say, just like before, and drop anything else that you might be doing to be with me."

I try to hide my excitement at the prospect of this, but I'm not too successful.

A wide smile starts to slip across my face.

"And, of course, you would have to call me Mr. Black again. And Sir. For the whole seven days."

My throat tightens up and becomes so parched that it feels like I haven't had a drop to drink in days.

"What do you think about that?"

"I don't know," I say, trying to keep my composure. "What's in it for me?"

"Well, besides the fact that I would pay you handsomely, you'd have the time of your life."

I don't want to be so crude, but I do want to know the amount. Little does he know, however, that I want him so much that I would probably do it for free.

"How does three hundred thousand sound?" he asks. "I know that I paid a quarter million for the night, but those were extenuating circumstances, weren't they?"

I feel the power dynamic between us shifting. He wants me. A lot.

"How about $500,000? That is still quite a discount given how much you paid just for one night."

"Wow, Ellie." Mr. Black seems to be taken quite aback by my negotiation skills. "I honestly didn't expect that. But, you know what? Why not? It's just money, right?"

I guess, I want to say.

"Okay, then. It's a deal. Half a million dollars. I'll pay you half now and half in a week."

"Sounds good."

"Now you know, I'm going to have to punish you a little for setting such a high price, right?"

"I'd expect nothing less," I say with a coy smile.

His eyes roll to the back of his head with pleasure.

My confidence is blowing his mind.

Of course, it's easier for me to be this confident, outgoing person over video.

He's not in the room with me.

He's not making me wet and making my whole body shudder with just one glance.

Let's see if he will be so impressed when we're back together again in the same room.

CHAPTER 21 - ELLIE

WHEN I GO OUT WITH MY FRIEND…

*M*r. Black transfers a quarter of a million dollars into my bank account within a few hours of our call.

Now, I have half a million dollars in there.

The amount seems mind-boggling and it doesn't feel real at all.

As for when the week actually starts, Mr. Black wants that to be a surprise.

My job is to go on with my days, doing whatever I was going to do and he is going to surprise me.

He's going to call me and ask me to meet him somewhere and I have to comply immediately.

The idea of him calling on me, requiring me to be somewhere, is a huge turn-on.

Of course, I would never put up with something like this in a real relationship.

But this isn't what this is.

This is a game. He wants me on certain terms, and I give myself up to him on certain terms.

As soon as Caroline gets home, she is already planning her night.

It's a long process that involves an hour long shower and a careful pairing of outfits and shoes.

She usually blasts the music and goes through ten outfits and calling me over and telling me that she has nothing to wear in her whole walk-in closet before deciding on the first dress that she tried on.

"Please, come out today. Pretty please?" Caroline pleads.

"Seriously?" I laugh. "I haven't heard that expression since the nineties."

"Well, you know me, I like to roll old school," she says, taking off a perfectly fine red dress and changing her bra and panties before trying on the next outfit. "But, seriously, just come out tonight. It will be so fun!"

After a few moments of debate, I finally cave.

I haven't been out to a proper club in a long time.

Caroline goes all the time, but I'm more of a homebody.

That's probably because her night doesn't even begin until eleven at night, and I'm usually in bed with a steamy romance on my Kindle by then.

"Yes!" Caroline jumps up and down and gives me a big hug. "I just met these girls today. They came into the gallery and bought a hundred thousand dollar painting for their new apartment on Park Avenue. They're loaded, of course."

Despite how much money Caroline has, she is still properly impressed when other people have money. Seriously, I thought she would be used to it by now.

I head to my own room and rifle through my less than lavish wardrobe to find something suitable to wear.

Unfortunately, I only have two pairs of club-appropriate shoes and two dresses.

I guess I could go for a pair of tight jeans, but the weather is still relatively warm and I want to soak up as much of the warmth as is still available to me before the cold, dark winter descends on Manhattan.

While looking through my clothes, something occurs to me.

I could have actually bought that painting from Caroline as well.

Not that I would spend that much on a painting.

In some parts of the country, a hundred grand buys a nice two bedroom house, but it is still an interesting thought to consider. Wow. Me. Imagine that!

Around ten thirty, Caroline is finally ready.

Waiting for her all evening, I managed to read half of a new hot romance that's burning up the charts on Amazon.

As an English major, romances are my guilty pleasure.

I love to get lost in the complexity of the relationships and the steamy sex scenes don't hurt much either.

Caroline doesn't really get them.

She thinks they're trash and limits her reading to what the traditional publishers like to refer to as literary fiction.

The only problem with that is that she barely reads at all while I manage to read a few books a week.

We meet Caroline's new friends at the end of the long line full of hopeful girls dressed in their Saturday night's best.

They are both blonde and bubbly and masters at walking on four-inch stiletto heels.

I, on the other hand, feel like I'm going to fall over at any moment.

The line is long, but it seems to move swiftly.

The bouncers make their judgments quickly and anyone who isn't the right size or isn't dressed well doesn't get in.

Single men have basically no hope at all.

Personally, I doubt that they'd even let me in if I wasn't with such a hot crowd.

The music inside the club is pumping, and the room is sweaty and hot.

The thing about clubbing in New York is that you can never bring a jacket or a coat with you, even when it's ten degrees outside, because no places have any coat checks and it's too hot inside to keep it on and too annoying to carry around with you. Luckily, the nights are still warm enough this early in the fall that it's not much of a consideration.

Caroline and the girls expertly position themselves at the bar and wait for some unsuspecting male to buy them a drink.

I'm about to get my own when Caroline stops me.

"Hey, what do you think you're doing?" she asks. "The cocktails here are fifteen bucks."

That's definitely not cheap, but at this point, I

don't really know if I care to make conversation with some guy in exchange for the drink.

My bank account is loaded, and my mind is occupied entirely by Mr. Black.

It has been more than a few hours since I made the agreement to be his for a week, and I don't know exactly when the week will officially begin.

To say that I'm waiting with anticipation would be an understatement.

"It's fine, honestly," I say. "Can I get an Old Fashioned, please?"

That's kind of a man's drink, but the taste of bitter orange is enticing.

Caroline and her friends just shake their heads.

It doesn't matter that they are wealthy all on their own. They are not the type to ever volunteer to pay for something when a man can do it for them.

When my drink arrives and Caroline is chatting up a hot investment banker type at the bar, my phone vibrates against my thigh. I glance at the screen.

It's Mr. Black.

Meet me at Avenue A and East Second Street.

10 minutes.

My heart skips a beat.

I don't know what's there, so I look up the
location on my phone.

But nothing really shows up.

Odd.

The only thing I know about that place is that
the Upright Citizen's Brigade is right around the
corner and I've been to that comedy club a number
of times and always had a really good time.

I tap Caroline on the shoulder and tell her that I
have go.

"Oh, no, why?"

"I have to see Mr. Black," I whisper into her ear.

"Really? Mr. Black?"

Her eyes grow wide and a big smile comes on
her face.

Clearly, my attempt to keep this info under
wraps was not successful.

"Who's Mr. Black?" The girls lean over
inquisitively.

"I'll tell you later," Caroline says.

"No, you won't. Because you promised,
remember?" I say admonishingly. "He's just a friend
of mine."

"Okay, okay, I won't say anything." Caroline
waves her hand. I don't really believe her, but I let
it go.

"Have fun!" the girls squeal with excitement. I roll my eyes.

I decide to walk over to Avenue A and East Second Street instead of calling a cab or using Uber.

It's an unseasonably warm night and New York is at its finest.

Within a few blocks, my feet start to pinch as I wobble along in my stilettos, but at this point, I'm too close to the place to bother with getting a cab.

Mr. Black is standing at the intersection, facing away from me.

My eyes land on his perfectly pert ass.

When he turns around, I see that his gorgeous body is dressed in an expertly tailored three-piece suit.

Watching me approach, his icy cold gaze melts and a small smile forms at the corners of his mouth.

I feel a crackling in the air that forms as I get closer and closer to him.

It's almost as if our bodies are putting off electricity. The sense of anticipation is deafening.

When I am within an arm's reach of him, we take a moment to examine each other. The man who is staring back at me is dark and dangerous and mine for the whole week.

I look up at his face and lose myself as if I'm in a

trance. His cheekbones look like they've been sculpted by Michelangelo, and his dark eyebrows make a perfect frame for his thickly lashed eyes.

His nose is prominent and strong to match his jaw and that mouth.

My knees grow weak at the memories of what they did to me last weekend.

Mr. Black takes me by the shoulders and pulls me closer to him.

When he presses his lips to mine, my whole body burns for him.

"Hey there, gorgeous," he whispers.

Lots of men use that phrase, but in their mouths it sounds trite and boring.

And like a lie.

But when Mr. Black says those words to me, I know that he's telling the truth.

"Are you ready for tonight?"

"That depends. What do you have planned?" I ask.

"Something very exciting," he says slowly and deliberately.

The tone of his voice sends shivers through my body.

I'm not a big fan of surprises, but so far Mr. Black

has gone far and above in giving me only the most pleasurable surprises.

He stares at me with such intensity that I start to feel faint.

I'm not yet used to the power of his gaze.

It's both distant, cold, and absolutely scorching hot.

Mr. Black takes my hand and leads me into a nondescript doorway, which looks like it leads to a small apartment building.

We ride the service elevator all the way to the top and when we get off, a substantial man with a clipboard meets us. He asks for our names and Mr. Black gives him his and says I'm his date.

The man smiles approvingly, checks him off, and points us to the door behind him.

"What is this place?" I ask.

"It's a private club."

CHAPTER 22 - ELLIE

WHEN THINGS GO TOO FAR...

I walk in holding Mr. Black's hand.

My own hand is clearly sweaty and I feel a little bit self-conscious about it.

But as much as I try to squirm away from him, he keeps a firm grip on me.

The room that we walk into is romantically lit.

The walls are padded and red, and the large chandeliers that descend from the ceiling put out a smooth, sensual light that reminds me of thousands of candles.

The people in this room are dressed pretty much like the people at the club.

Women are in high heels and short dresses, tossing their hair with extensions from one side to the other.

The men are dressed in tailored suits and look like they just walked out of the boardroom.

No one looks older than forty-five.

At the far corner of the room is the bar and Mr. Black takes me straight there.

He orders a glass of the top-shelf whiskey for himself and a Cosmopolitan for me.

The light pink drink in the elegant martini glass makes me feel elegant and sophisticated.

Walking in on the arm of Mr. Black doesn't hurt things either.

"So, what's so special about this private club?" I ask, taking a sip and looking around.

I've heard of private clubs before.

Caroline, for instance, is dying to get into the SoHo House. Besides the exclusive people who are in there and the pool you can use on hot New York summer days, I'm not really sure what value it really offers.

Mr. Black winks at me, but doesn't answer.

"Is it one of those stuffy country clubs?" I ask. "Like they have in the Hamptons? I've been there and they're not amazing."

He shakes his head and smiles.

"It has something of a different vibe," Mr. Black says, squeezing my hand. My heart skips a beat.

"Follow me."

Grabbing my drink, I follow him into another room. And that's when I come face-to-face with another world.

There are people having sex everywhere.

On the couches, on the desks, on the bar. Some are in couples, but most are in groups of three. I glance at Mr. Black with a horrified look on my face, but he meets my look with a smile and a shrug.

"It's a sex club," he whispers. "We don't have to participate necessarily, but it would be more fun."

I drop his hand. Suddenly, the person that I thought I knew dissipates and I stand face-to-face with a stranger.

Without a word, I turn around and run out.

Mr. Black follows me.

I don't stop at the bar; instead, I go all the way outside before he manages to grab my hand and swing me around.

"What's wrong?" he asks.

His eyes are wide and perplexed.

He actually has no idea that he's done anything wrong bringing me there.

"What did you think was going to happen in there?" I ask.

"I don't know. I thought we would have some fun."

"Well, that's not my idea of fun."

"I don't understand," Mr. Black says, shaking his head. I can see it in his eyes that he's actually at a loss. But I don't care. I'm angry.

"I have to go," I say.

"But what about our agreement?"

"Are you fucking kidding me? You can have the money back. I don't care. You had no right to ask me to go there."

"How's this any different than the show we watched on the yacht?"

"It's completely different...We weren't right there, for one," I say. I search my mind for more differences, but besides the fact that there was a glass, I have trouble coming up with any. Shit.

"I don't know," I add. "It just is."

I want to cry.

It takes all of my energy to keep my true feelings to myself.

I flag down a cab and get in without saying another word.

As soon as the cab pulls away, I burst out in tears.

I don't know what has come over me, but for

some reason this whole experience feels completely different than what happened at the yacht.

I'm still crying when the cab pulls up to my apartment. I hand the driver my credit card and barely see what I'm writing when I sign my name.

This was not how the night was supposed to go.

There was supposed to be more to this.

As I wash my face and wipe the eyeliner and mascara off my eyes, it finally hits me. The real reason why I got so upset was that I was expecting so much more.

I didn't even know it, but I had actually developed feelings for Mr. Black. No, I shouldn't even call him that.

His real name is Aiden.

I mean, I actually thought that because he shared his real name with me, and he wanted to see me again, that meant that he was actually into me.

How stupid is that?

I feel like such a fool.

I walk around my apartment, lost in thought.

I turn on the television so I don't feel so alone, but I still can't keep all of these thoughts from swirling around in my head.

I keep thinking back to last weekend.

He toyed with me and pleasured me in a way
that I'd never experienced before.

He put off his pleasure to please me.

He punished me for orgasming first and I
liked that.

I wanted all that again.

And again.

I've never met a man like him before. It's not just
that he's rich.

He's also mysterious and in control.

He embodies power and there's something
intoxicating about that.

I sit down at my laptop and try to relive what
happened on the yacht.

In the story, I'm about ten thousand words in and
I'm just about to be auctioned off.

I sit staring at the screen for a long time, but no
words come.

Unlike in the beginning, when the words just
poured out of me, this time, nothing comes.

When I think back to the auction, I am no longer
excited.

Instead, I'm disappointed and angry.

I'm angry at what just happened and that my
expectations of Aiden didn't conform to reality.

I slam my laptop screen shut and go to the kitchen.

In the fridge, I find a brand new, unopened pint of Ben & Jerry's Chocolate Cherry Garcia.

It's my absolute favorite.

I'm actually surprised that it's not half gone since it's Caroline's favorite, too.

I climb into bed with the pint and a spoon.

The tension in the back of my neck doesn't let up until the first drop lands on my tongue.

A few spoonfuls later, the tears finally stop flowing.

I flip on the television in my room and focus my attention on *The Real Housewives of New York City*.

This show and all of its spinoffs have been my guilty pleasure for as long as I can remember.

There is something mind-numbing and saccharine about it that it makes me feel like no matter how shitty my life is at least I don't have their problems.

Sometime in the middle of the episode, when I'm nearly halfway through my pint of ice cream, I hear Caroline come home.

She's talking loudly and laughing and clearly pretty intoxicated.

I'm about to go out to say hi when I hear a male voice.

I turn down the television, but I still can't quite make out what they're saying, but I can hear them laughing.

One of them flips off the television in the living room and then they start to make out.

The sounds of kissing quickly morph into the sounds of lovemaking as Caroline starts to moan loudly while she's being slammed against what sounds like the kitchen island.

None of this is new to me.

I'm used to this, of course.

We have known each other since Yale and she has been quite open about her sex life for many years.

Some people, who I would never associate with, would call her a slut.

But I hate that word.

It's sexist because it only applies to women who have a lot of sex.

A man in her position is just a man who likes sex.

A single man in his early twenties.

What else does the world expect him to do?

That's what I think of Caroline's sex life as well.

She's an empowered modern woman who has sex whenever, and with whomever, she pleases.

Just when they are about to finish, my phone goes off.

I look at the screen.

It's Aiden.

I click ignore and put it away.

I don't want to hear anything he has to say.

Apparently, I was wrong about where we stood and that's fine. But he keeps calling.

Again and again and again.

When my phone beeps, showing that there's a voicemail message, I can't help but listen to it.

"Ellie, I'm so sorry. I really didn't mean to offend you. Please answer the phone. I really need to apologize to you."

I click delete and the second voicemail message pops up.

"Ellie, please answer. I know you're there. I was such a dick. Please let me explain. I'm sorry."

Four more messages follow, basically saying the same thing.

A part of me wants to talk to him.

But another part is still angry and hurt even though I'm not really hurt and angry at him.

After finishing my pint of ice cream, my thoughts are clearer now.

I'm hurt because I'm an idiot.

I was the one who developed all of these expectations of him that he, or any other man, couldn't possibly live up to.

I mean, what the hell was I thinking?

I met him a few days ago at a fucking auction for sex.

How could I expect a man who spends his time paying exorbitant amounts of money for girls to spend the night with him to actually have feelings for me?

And to make our relationship anything but what it is?

Just sex?

And why do I even want to have a relationship with him?

Actually, I don't.

Not at all.

I mean, I really liked all those things he did to me that night, but that doesn't mean that we have anything in common.

He's really hot, and his body is to die for, but I'm not that shallow, right?

I mean, I'm not Caroline.

And speaking of Caroline?

Why can't I just be more like her?

Why can't I just enjoy the sexual pleasures that life has to offer without becoming some sappy little love struck girl?

There's more to life than relationships and love.

There's fun and pleasure and just having a good time.

And there's nothing wrong with that.

And with all of these thoughts swirling around in my head, I flip off the light and lie down to go to sleep before the ice cream induced sugar coma has the chance to hit me.

CHAPTER 23 - MR. BLACK

WHEN I CAN'T GET HER OUT OF MY MIND...

I don't really understand what just happened.

Why did Ellie freak out like that at the club?

How's that place any different from what we watched back at the yacht?

There were people having sex right in front of us and she was turned on and totally game for anything.

Maybe she's not the girl that I thought she was after all.

And yet, for some reason, I can't seem to get her out of my head.

Fuck me.

I mean, I didn't really expect her to join in with everyone. I know that it was her first time.

But I thought that we would at least watch some of the show and then retreat to one of the private rooms for our own good time.

Still, it serves me right, I guess, for just assuming things about this almost stranger I've only just met.

The one thing I should've known for sure is that she's not like all those other girls.

She's different.

Maybe that's why I'm so attracted to her.

She isn't eager to please me or make me laugh.

She has her own opinions about things and she isn't afraid to share them.

Oh, how easy it would be to just go for all those normal bimbos that are usually my type.

They're so much less...complicated.

After watching her drive away in the cab, I turn around and head back inside the club.

If she doesn't want to join me, that's her problem. The place is swarming with hot horny girls who would do anything to be with me.

I order an Old Fashioned at the bar and swirl around on my bar stool to examine the prospects.

Club Aura is definitely not your run of the mill social club.

Not only is it incredibly expensive, it's also very

exclusive and the owners are very good at letting in just the right type of people to make this place pop.

I scan the room for a possible conquest. There's a six foot blonde in the corner that flutters her eyelashes at me. She has large breasts, which are spilling out of her corset and they are definitely a sight for tired eyes. When I give her a slight nod, that's all the invitation she needs.

Much to my surprise, however, she doesn't come over alone. She walks over with a brunette, who is an inch or two taller than she is with legs so long they go up all the way to my chest.

"Well, hello, darlings," I say, flashing them my famous crooked smile that makes the ladies swoon.

"Hey, stranger," the brunette says.

They introduce themselves and I repeat the names in my head so that I don't forget.

But I know tomorrow they will be nothing but a blur and the only way I'll differentiate between the two is by their hair color.

"We were just wondering if you would like to join us in a private room?" The blonde smiles at me, running her manicured fingers over my forearm. My dick reacts almost immediately.

"Yes, of course."

A private room in the club is not really all that private, but that's part of the fun.

The doors always stay open, and each room has a large California King bed to fit three, four, or six people depending on your desires.

There are also couches and love seats nearby, if you really want to make it a party.

The one the hostess shows us to has a large glass window, giving us a clear view of the seven person orgy going on on the other side.

The people make a chain, linking their asses and their lips.

The sight makes me hard and also makes my heart ache a little.

Why couldn't I be here with Ellie instead?

Why did she have to be so against this? The fact that there's a woman out there who I can't have makes me cringe.

The brunette turns to the blonde and pulls her onto the bed.

She immediately goes for her luscious breasts, pulling one after the other out of her corset. While she kisses her nipples, the blonde reaches out to me and pulls me over by grabbing my pants.

"Don't be shy," she whispers and starts to unzip my fly.

I close my eyes and try to lose myself in the moment.

Normally, it's that easy. I have two hot girls who are going to do crazy sexy things in front of me and with me.

But, in this moment, I suddenly feel different.

My mind is going a million different directions, and I can't focus myself no matter what I do.

I open my eyes and watch as the girl unbuttons my shirt and runs her fingernails down my six pack.

"You like this, baby?" she whispers, licking her lips and getting down on her knees. My cock is hard and ready to go, but my mind isn't.

All I can see is Ellie.

All I can think about is how much I wish she were Ellie instead.

Suddenly, my erection starts to disappear. Before I go entirely limp, I pull away.

"What's wrong?"

"Nothing."

"Oh, c'mon, I'll get you back up," she says, grabbing at me.

I shake my head no and push her hands off me.

"I'm sorry, but I can't do this now," I say.

I am as surprised by the words that just came out of my mouth as the girls are.

Their eyes widen in disbelief. They crowd around me and try to convince me to stay. But I pull away and walk out.

All I want is Ellie right now.

I want to touch her, kiss her, and wrap my arms around her.

Waiting for my car at the valet, I think about the chump that I've become.

I'm actually one of those guys who would turn down a threesome with two ridiculously hot chicks in exchange for some other girl who doesn't seem to want anything to do with me.

Fuck me!

Who the hell am I becoming?

When my car arrives and I give the valet a rather generous tip, I dial Ellie's number on my cell phone.

The call goes straight to voicemail.

I debate whether I should leave one and eventually do.

I know she has her phone on her and is just not picking up.

This makes me angry so I call again and leave another message.

When she doesn't pick up again, I see red.

I want to scream at her.

Why won't she accept my apology?

How can she not understand that it was just a mistake?

I'm sorry, okay?

I want to scream into the phone.

But I don't.

I leave another apology.

It's more urgent than the others, but I don't dare let her see my anger.

That won't do me any good.

Besides, I'm not angry at her.

The person I'm really angry with is myself.

I took a nice girl, who I really like, for granted.

I pushed her boundaries.

That club isn't for everyone.

Why the hell would I think it would be okay to take her there?

Riding the elevator up to my penthouse, I feel like such a fool.

A confused fool.

I mean, why the hell is Ellie so special?

Why am I so drawn to her?

To be completely honest, she's got pretty average looks. And a normal body. Not too thin, not too voluptuous, nothing too special.

They will definitely not put her on the cover of Vogue anytime soon. There are about a million girls who are way hotter and more sexually adventurous in the tri-state area than she is.

I don't really know anything about what she's really like.

What kind of music does she like?

What kind of movies?

Do we even have anything in common at all?

And yet...I can't stop thinking about her.

CHAPTER 24 - ELLIE

WHEN A FRIEND RETURNS…

The following morning, I wake up with a knock at the door.

It takes me a moment to remember where I am because my head is pounding from all the sugar that I consumed the night before.

My eyes are dry and feel like they're being cut with razor blades. My mouth feels like a parched desert. I lick my chapped lips and stumble out of my room.

In the living room, I hear the knock at the door getting more insistent.

Who the hell could that be this early?

I glance at the clock.

Well, it's after ten, but still.

Who just shows up at the door anymore nowadays?

I look into the peep hole and see that it's Tom.

"What do you want?" I ask, opening the door.

"I need to talk to you."

"I don't want to talk to you," I say.

"Listen, I'm here to apologize. I'm really sorry about everything I said."

I try to close the door, but he puts his foot in the door frame.

"Okay, that's fine," I say. "But I still don't want to talk now."

"Not good," he says, dropping his shoulders. "I had a fight with Carrie."

I look him up and down.

He looks pathetic.

Like a lost puppy dog.

I can't help but empathize with him.

Despite what he said to me, we have been friends for a very long time.

And I both hate and love him for that.

"I need to talk to you, Ellie. Please," he says, looking straight into my eyes.

A few strands of his hair fall into his eyes, giving him a sultry mysterious look, which always makes my heart melt.

No, I have to be strong. I'm tired of his bullshit.
I'm over him.

"I'm really, really sorry. I didn't mean any of that.
I just...didn't want you to quit. Who the hell am I
going to talk to in that place now?"

Agh, how can I say no to that face?

His eyes look up at me with that begging look on
his face.

"Fine." I finally cave.

I glance in the mirror as I let Tom in.

My hair is a total mess.

That whole loose bun phenomenon that's so
popular online makes me look like I haven't
showered in days.

I'm not wearing a stitch of makeup, and I have a
large zit near my right temple. It's not that I want to
look good for Tom.

It's just that I always make myself put on at least
some concealer, eyeliner, and mascara before
releasing myself into the world. There's a confidence
that comes with makeup as armor.

But I guess I don't have that luxury this morning.

I pour him a cup of coffee and wait.

We used to spend hours talking to one another.

And now, he seems more like a stranger to me
than a friend. I try to remember when it all changed.

"Listen, I'm sorry again. Okay? I was a total jerk," Tom says, taking a sip. "You quitting just caught me off guard."

"Yeah, I know," I say with a shrug.

"So, what are you going to do now?"

"Actually, I'm working on a story. A novel maybe. I don't know."

"What kind?"

At Yale, Tom was always the person who listened to writing problems.

He was the one who always supported me.

He was the one I used to turn to whenever I got rejection slips from literary journals.

"It's actually something a little different. From everything else that I ever wrote, I mean."

"Oh, yeah? That's intriguing. What's it about?"

A part of me doesn't really want to tell him.

He doesn't know anything about Mr. Black or what happened at the yacht party except for the fact that I went there.

Frankly, I don't really know if I should keep it that way or not.

"I'll tell you later," I say, buying myself some time. "What's going on with Carrie?"

"I don't know. This whole wedding is making her nuts."

I nod.

"A Valentine's Day wedding sounds nice."

"I guess. Except that it's in the middle of February and not exactly wedding season. Her parents aren't exactly pleased. And since they're paying for it...I don't know. It's just annoying. There's a bit too much family drama for me."

I don't really know how to respond to this.

It's no surprise that I don't really like Carrie, but that doesn't mean anything. Not really.

"But you love her right?" I ask.

"Yes, of course," he answers a little bit too quickly. "I'm just starting to think that maybe we rushed into this."

"Yeah, you just started dating last January, right?"

He nods.

"You know, don't take this wrong, but I just thought that you would take it a little slower. I mean, you haven't had many relationships before this."

"I know. But when we got together, it was such a whirlwind. And we got along so well. I wanted to ask her to marry me because it just felt so right."

Ah, the fated engagement.

I remember that night very well.

It was as much of a surprise to me as Carrie.

It was the night of our graduation.

Carrie had graduated a few years before, but she was there to watch Tom walk across the stage.

We got together with a bunch of our friends for what I thought would be a night of debauchery and excess drinking.

But then, right in the middle of the party, Tom turned to Carrie and asked her to marry him.

And she fucking said yes.

There was a lot of debauchery and drinking on my part after that, but not to celebrate anything, that's for sure.

"I thought I would ask her to marry me and then we would have a long engagement. Like a year or two before we even started talking wedding plans. But she called her parents and her mom hired a wedding planner that weekend."

"Wow, I didn't know that."

"Yeah, you weren't really around for that," he says with reproach. "Why was that?"

"What do you mean?"

"I mean, you were my best friend in college. And then when I started dating Carrie, things just sort of went awry with us."

"Do you really not know?"

He shrugs.

Well, I might as well tell him now.

"I had feelings for you, Tom. I thought I was in love with you for like two years."

"You did? But you never said anything!"

"Well, I was going to, but then you and Carrie started dating," I say, tactically trying to avoid bringing up that one failed kiss that he planted on me after my own two-year relationship fell apart and I wasn't ready for a rebound - let alone a rebound with such a good friend.

"I just don't fucking know how life got so complicated, Ellie. I mean, things seemed to be so much less complex when we were in school. Didn't they?"

"Yeah, they did. But then again, it was college. We didn't have jobs or responsibilities. Or fiancées."

"Carrie's parents are buying us a two-bedroom apartment on Park Avenue as our wedding present."

"Wow, that must be nice."

"It is and it isn't. I mean, I like where I live."

"But you don't expect her to move into your shitty studio where the plumbing and the air conditioner don't work half the time," I say. "I mean, her parents make your dad look like he's a pauper."

Tom shrugs and looks away.

"Listen, Tom, don't get so upset. Having lots of money isn't that bad," I say, putting my arm around him. "I mean, most people just dream of the life that you have."

"I know, but I don't."

I know exactly what he's worried about. I've known him way too long.

"You're not going to become a sellout automatically just by moving to Park Avenue. Besides, who knows, maybe this will give you the time and space to actually focus on your writing career."

"Yeah, maybe," he says, unconvinced.

"You want to write about politics, right? Well, marrying a rich girl will give you all the money you will ever need to go on the campaign trail and really report on what's going on on the front lines."

"Except that Carrie and her father have other plans for me. They want me to go into corporate. He wants to take me under his wing and groom me for taking over BuzzPost."

"Oh, wow, that's...something."

"It's something alright. Except that I don't want to be some corporate drone, Ellie. I want to write what I want to write. The whole reason I even took this job at BuzzPost was so that I could maybe get the chance to write some of their political pieces."

"Well, you can talk to Carrie about this, right? I mean, she is the editor."

Tom shakes his head and turns away from me.

"It's not all her decision. She's an only child and she isn't interested in taking over the company in the future. Her dad is looking for someone within the family."

I don't know what to say so I go to make another pot of coffee.

Just as I'm about to turn around, I feel someone right behind me.

Tom leans down, turning my face up to his.

Then he presses his lips onto mine and inhales lightly.

Two years ago, our first kiss was all wrong, but this one isn't much better.

This moment feels entirely forced and wrong.

"What are you doing?" I pull away immediately.

"I want you, Ellie," he whispers, nearly on the verge of tears.

"You're engaged. And I'm..."

"What?"

"I'm with someone. Sort of."

It's hard to quite explain what Mr. Black and I are except that I would give anything for him to be here instead of Tom right now.

"That's not good enough, Ellie. We belong together. Don't you see that?"

"Tom, we're friends. You're engaged. I'm here for you, but I can't be with you. I don't want to be. You need to figure out what you're doing with Carrie first."

"And if I break up with her?"

"What?! How can you even say that?"

"Do we have a chance if I break up with her?"

"I can't believe you're asking me that," I say. "No, of course not. I don't feel this way toward you anymore, Tom."

"That's a lie," he mumbles, but I can tell he isn't completely convinced.

"I'm over you, Tom. You need to figure out what you want to do with Carrie on your own. But don't take me into consideration in that decision at all."

Though I don't feel the same way about Tom anymore, I'm not entirely sure that what I'm saying is completely true.

What I am sure about is that I don't need to be involved with his whole Carrie mess right now.

And I'm also positive that I want to see Mr. Black - also known as Aiden - again, despite what happened between us.

Tom pulls away from me and pours himself

another cup of coffee.

"So, tell me about your writing."

I want him to leave, but I also want to turn the page.

And if I ask him to leave now, the failed kiss will always be there, a big elephant in the room.

Maybe changing the topic now isn't such a bad idea after all.

"I don't really know what to say." I shrug. "I really want to take this time off work and try to figure things out for myself. Mainly, what sort of things I want to write."

"So what did you come up with?"

"It's actually kind of different. It's about sex."

"Really?" Tom chuckles.

"What's so funny?"

"You're just not the type, I guess," he says, smiling.

"Like you would know."

"Well, I mean, it's just a departure from your normal writing, that's all."

Tom is the only person who has ever read all of my writing.

I've been writing for as long as I can remember, even as a little kid.

I wrote a number of fan fiction stories when I

was a teenager and was in love with Twilight and Harry Potter. But it wasn't until Yale that I started to write more serious things.

I devoured literary magazines with the zest of a starving woman and wrote stories that I thought would be a good fit there.

Mostly, they were about mundane things – you know, the type in which not much happened – but it had all of this significance below the surface. Tom offered me a lot of good criticism and suggestions, but still none of them resulted in any publication, let alone any money.

"It's not just about sex. It's a romance about a girl who falls for a hot, wealthy man," I say.

"A romance novel?"

"Yeah. I've been reading a lot on my Kindle recently and I think that would be the best way to describe it."

"Seriously?" He laughs.

"Listen, I know it's not the highbrow that I worked on before. But those stories didn't see the light of day. They took like a month of work for a two-thousand word story and for what? No one ever saw them, let alone read them, or paid any money for them. All I have to show for them is a pile of rejection slips."

"And you think this story has more potential?"

"Yes, I do. It's really in line with what I've read on Amazon. Besides, it's kind of fun to write about sex. All those juicy details. It's really indulgent."

"Okay," Tom says, shaking his head and raising his eyebrows. "Hey, you don't need my permission, of course."

"No, I don't," I confirm. "What? What is it with that face?"

"Nothing. I guess it's my own bias, but I never thought that you would be the one reading, let alone, writing trashy romance novels."

"That's kind of elitist, don't you think? Even a bit prejudiced?"

"Why?"

"Because you've never read a romance novel in your life. And you're here making all kinds of statements about it and the people who read them. They're just for fun. They're an escape. A fantasy. They're no different than fantasy novels or page-turning thrillers. And what's it to you anyway, if I'm having a good time writing it?"

Tom considers this for a moment and finally caves.

"I guess you're right. It's your writing. You can write whatever you want."

"Yes, I can."

"So, not to bring up money again, but are you going to live off Mitch again?" Tom asks after a moment. Oh, shit. Here's the topic of money again. For someone who pretends not to care about money, it sure does creep into every conversation.

"No, but why do you care?"

"You won't? Did you find some holy grail where you can write whatever you want and still pay your own bills?"

"Listen, I'm going to tell you something, but promise that you won't get mad, okay?" I say.
He nods.

"Well, last weekend, at the yacht party, I met someone," I say.

I choose my words carefully as I'm not entirely sure if I want to reveal everything that happened there.

Not yet, anyway. Tom doesn't say anything and just waits for me to continue.

"They had this game there. Kind of like a sex game."

"What?!" he gasps.

"Listen, everything is okay. It was fun actually. It was an auction. The girls were basically auctioned off for a night of...whatever. But you didn't have to participate unless you wanted to. It was all in good fun."

As soon as the words escape my mouth, I immediately regret bringing any of it up at all.

The look on Tom's face says everything.

"Wait, so let me get this straight. You auctioned yourself off to the highest bidder. Had sex with this creep all night and now you have enough money to not work and do whatever the hell you want?"

"It was just a game, Tom. All in good fun. And he wasn't a creep. Not at all."

"Any guy who would pay for a woman like that is a John, Ellie."

"You think that? And what does that make me then?" I ask.

"Hey, I'm not afraid to say it."

"Are you calling me a whore? Are you seriously doing that right now?"

"If the definition fits."

"Fuck you, Tom. Get the fuck out of my house! Now."

"Listen, I'm sorry." Tom starts to walk back some of what he said. But I'm in no mood to listen to any of it.

"I need you to leave," I say, opening the front door and waiting for him to leave.

CHAPTER 25 - ELLIE

I slam the door shut as soon as Tom leaves.

I hate him for what he has said.

Why does he have to be such an asshole?

I know that he's going through his own shit, but that doesn't mean that he has to make me feel so bad.

Suddenly, all the things that I should've said and could've said come to me.

This is one of my main issues.

When I get insulted, I often find myself at a loss for words. I'm so shocked by what the other person just said that I don't respond at all.

I did kick him out, but there is so much more that I should've said back to him.

Like, 'what about you? You act like you don't care about money but you're marrying one of the richest women in New York?'

And, at least I like Aiden.

What about you?

You're engaged and you're out there trying to pick up your friend because deep down you can't stand the sight of her.

The ring of my phone breaks up my train of thought. I look at the screen.

It's Mr. Black.

Again.

This must be his seventh call since last night.

I consider not taking it, but my finger presses the accept call button before I'm able to stop myself.

"Hello?"

"Ellie? Is that you?"

His voice is rushed, frantic even.

Worried.

This isn't Mr. Black calling.

This is the man behind the mystery.

It's Aiden.

"What do you want, Aiden?" I ask.

"I don't know if you got all of my other messages, but I just wanted to apologize again. I'm sorry that I took you there. I honestly didn't know it was going to be a problem. But I should've known."

"Okay," I say slowly.

"Can I make it up to you?"

"Listen, Aiden, I can give you back your money."

"I don't give a fuck about money."

"I just don't think this whole lifestyle is for me. The yacht was fun, but I think it's too much."

"I totally understand. We're moving too fast."

"I don't know if I'll ever want to do that. I think we just want different things."

There's a long pause on the other end.

"Ellie, I just want to get to know you better. That's all. That club was too much. I know that now. But can I just take you out on a normal date? Dinner? Nothing else? Just so we can get to know each other better."

"Just dinner?" I ask. "No strings attached. No Mr. Black?"

"No, no Mr. Black. Just a dinner date with me, Aiden Black."

I think about this for a second.

I definitely like the sound of that.

Aiden and I have amazing sexual chemistry, but that night on the yacht just made me want to get to know him a bit better.

Who is the real Aiden Black?

"Okay," I say after a moment. "Okay."

"Okay? Great. How about tomorrow night at seven? I'll pick you up at your place."

"Wow, this is going to be a traditional date, huh?"

"That's exactly what I promised. And I keep my promises."

———

THE DAY PASSES in a blur as I try to figure out what I should wear.

My wardrobe isn't as big or diverse as Caroline's, so I raid her closet.

Like many friends and roommates, our closets tend to combine and become one except that my clothes tend to be a lot cheaper than hers.

I try on three different little black dresses and four different heels. I've never been a fan of heels, but I can't lie, I do love how they make my legs look. I try on a couple of pairs of skinny jeans and fancy blouses. I'm always much more comfortable in pants than I am in dresses, and with a nice flowing top, the jeans don't look so pedestrian. Plus, they do make my butt look quite good.

Finally, I settle on a pair of tight skinny jeans,

four-inch pumps, and a bright red blouse that makes my breasts pop.

Now, what the hell do I do with my hair?

I look at my shoulder length straight straw-like tresses that tend to fall flat around my face. I washed it earlier today, and air dried it, which made some strands separate and curl in odd ways. I run a brush through it and get my straightener out.

After applying some heat and curling the ends a bit to soften my look, I decide that I'm pretty much done with fussing about my hair.

That's the thing about straight blonde hair.

If you don't do much with it, people think you're going for the tossed beach look, which works for me.

After applying some concealer and foundation, eyeliner and accentuating my brows with some eyebrow liner, I put on a coat of mascara.

I look in the mirror.

Yeah, this looks about right.

Pretty, but not too dressed up.

Just in case this whole thing blows up in my face, I didn't put that much effort into looking like a million bucks.

That has always been my motto about getting dressed up. I never want to be the most dressy person in the room.

Unlike Caroline, who likes to take any opportunity to wear the fanciest of dresses, I'd rather look a little underdressed.

I hate looking like I'm trying too hard.

It's my armor against the world - to always be a little bit of an underachiever.

My doorbell rings precisely at seven.

I press the buzzer and wait for him to come upstairs.

Standing by the door, I start to shake.

I'm petrified.

We're no longer playing games.

This isn't some mysterious stranger coming to see me.

It's Aiden, not Mr. Black.

For some reason, the character of Mr. Black made me feel safe.

With him, I felt like I was playing a role and he was playing a role and, as long as we played those roles, we couldn't hurt each other.

Not in any real way.

Because the world was our stage and our relationship was just pretend.

An elaborate play in which we had starring roles.

I open the door when I hear his knock.

My hands are ice-cold, and I'm shivering even though it's pretty warm in the apartment.

"Hey," Aiden says softly, lowering his chin a little and letting the loose strands of his dark hair fall into his gorgeous almond-shaped eyes.

"Hey," I whisper back.

I'm so nervous that my heart feels like it's going to jump out of my chest.

"Are you ready?"

I nod, grab my purse, and lock the door.

While we wait for the elevator, Aiden reaches for my hand and squeezes it lightly.

When I look up at him, he flashes a big beautiful smile.

His skin is tan and his face is angular with a strong jaw and luscious pink lips.

When he licks them, I get chills.

"Not to bring up what happened again, but I just wanted to apologize again. In person," he says. "I was out of line for taking you there."

"It's okay," I mumble and follow him into the elevator. "I'm sorry I got so upset."

"You had every right to."

When we get downstairs, he leads me to his brand-new Tesla and opens the door for me.

The interior is the most luxurious car I've ever

been inside of. It smells like a new car and feels like one, too.

As we pull away from the curb, I see people staring at us.

You'd think that people in this part of Manhattan, and in Manhattan in general, would be used to seeing $125,000 cars driving around, but it still draws looks.

The windows are tinted so I stare back at them without worrying about meeting their eyes.

"Where are we going?" I ask.

"You'll see," Aiden says, winking at me.

He looks amazing behind the wheel.

His perfectly tailored suit hugs every curve and muscle without riding up or making him a bit frumpy.

For a moment, as we whiz down the somewhat empty streets completely impervious to the world that's going on around us, I feel like we're in a car commercial.

Everything about him is perfect and I don't want to make a sound to break the magic of this moment.

We turn onto Fifth Avenue and pull over to the steps of a building that I know very well.

It's the New York Public Library.

"What are we doing here?" I ask.

This is a no-parking zone, but Aiden turns off the engine and gets out of the car.

I look out of my window and see a bright red carpet going down the majestic steps, leading all the way to the car. Aiden gives me his hand to help me out of the car.

"No, seriously," I say. "What are we doing here? Do you have an overdue library book?"

He smiles coyly. "We're having dinner here."

"Here?" I ask as he leads me up the red carpet and to the top of the marble stairs.

He leads me past the two massive stone lions, dubbed Patience and Fortitude by the former mayor of New York, Fiorello La Guardia. They guard the main portal as if they are doing it with their lives.

"This is my favorite place in New York," I say.

"Really?"

"Yes, I've always loved libraries and this one...it just takes the cake. I've been here a million times before. Spent countless hours in the stacks and the reading room, especially when I was going through something hard."

"Well, it's one of my favorite places, too," he says, much to my own surprise. I didn't think that a CEO of a tech company would have much time to read for pleasure. "It's beautiful and majestic, isn't it? That's why I wanted to take you here."

"I had no idea," I whisper.

"The Rose Main Reading Room is one of my favorite places to go to get away from it all," Aiden says, squeezing my hand.

"Is that where we're headed now?" I ask.

He shakes his head.

"No, I have a little surprise for you."

I walk beside him as he leads me to the Celeste Bartos Forum, which is covered entirely by elegant flower displays.

I don't know anything about flowers or the different types of flowers, but the room looks like it has been set up for a wedding.

It has beautiful light pink and purple lighting around the accents of the room, drawing attention to the thirty-foot-high glass saucer domestic ceiling.

"This is beautiful," I whisper.

In the middle of the sixty four hundred square foot space sits a large table with a setting for two.

"I feel like we're crashing someone's party," I say.

"We're not. This is all for us," Aiden says.

I shake my head.

I feel a pang in my chest and I know that a

stream of tears is not far behind. I take a deep breath and try to keep them at bay.

"Are you okay?" Aiden looks me straight in my eyes.

"No. I mean yes. I've just never had anyone do anything like this for me before."

"I wanted our date to be special," he says.

"I thought we were going to go to some fancy restaurant, I didn't think you were going to book the New York Public Library for Christ's sake."

"If you don't like this, we can go somewhere else," he says quickly.

"No, you don't understand. This is...this is more than anyone else has ever done for me. It's beautiful. It's just...so much. I feel like I'm underdressed."

Aiden looks me up and down and shakes his head.

"No, you're perfect. You are the most beautiful woman in the world right now."

My cheeks get hot from embarrassment and I have to look away.

He takes my hand and leads me to the table.

He pulls the chair away for me and then slides it under.

When he positions himself across from me, I

watch as the candles dance in his deep eyes and I lose myself in the moment.

The waiter, dressed in an impeccable white tux, comes over with a towel across his arm.

I never knew what they were for, except to make them look very official.

He asks us what we would like to drink and Aiden orders a bottle of wine for us. I don't know much about wine, but the waiter seems impressed by his choice.

"I hope it's okay that I ordered for you," he says. "You just have to try this wine. It's amazing."

"Yes, it's fine. I'm kind of a dunce when it comes to wine. That's why I tend to just go for mojitos and margaritas at bars."

"If you'd prefer that, I can get you that."

"Oh, no, this is perfect," I say.

CHAPTER 26 - ELLIE

*a*t dinner, I lose myself in Aiden's eyes.

He looks at me like I'm the only girl in the world that matters.

I don't remember the last time anyone ever looked at me that way.

Or maybe no one ever has.

At first, we don't talk about much of substance, but then he asks me about my job.

I don't know what to say and consider lying. Except that I don't want to lie to him.

Not about anything.

"I don't work there anymore," I say, taking a bite of my salmon, which is so perfectly cooked that it practically melts in my mouth.

"You don't?"

"I quit. I hated my boss and when I had the money from that night...I sort of thought, why the hell would I subject myself to her anymore?"

"I like the sound of that," he says, smiling.

"You like the sound of unemployment?"

"No, I like the sound of a woman pursuing her dreams."

I blush. "What makes you think that that's what I'm doing?"

"I don't know. But I have a feeling. You love to write. And that sort of thing tends to eat at you if you don't do it."

How did he know so much about me? It's like he looked into my soul and it gave him access to all of my deepest and darkest secrets.

"So, what made you so smart?" I ask.

He shrugs and looks away. That ever-present twinkle in his eyes seems to vanish for a moment.

"What?" I press.

"I just know a creative person when I see one," he says after a moment. "There was a time, a long time ago, when I was interested in something other than computers, too."

"Really?" I sit up a little. "Like what?"

"Actually, I liked to paint," he says. "Watercolors, but sometimes with oil, too. It started with drawing, but I wanted to make a little bit more of a mess than colored pencils permitted me to."

"Wow, I had no idea," I whisper.

I'm actually taken aback by this.

On the surface, Aiden Black is a put-together, alpha billionaire with a big company to run and oversee. He's practically the last person you would ever imagine painting in their spare time.

"So, do you still paint?" I ask.

"Sometimes, late at night. When I can't sleep," he says. "Unfortunately, I don't have much time for hobbies."

"See, that's what I thought, too," I say. "Until a certain someone told me that there are some things in the world that are more important than money and a job."

Aiden throws his head back as he chuckles.

"What's the matter? You don't like someone throwing your own advice back at you?"

"No, it's not that. It's just that I don't just have a job. I run a whole company. Owl's main competitor is Amazon - so it's not even any small business either. And actually, I really like doing it. Painting - it's a passion, of course, but not as much as Owl."

I nod. I can see in his eyes that he's telling the truth.

When the waiter arrives with the dessert menu, I shake my head no and say that I'm too full.

"Okay, how about we get dessert to go?" Aiden asks. "Their chocolate mousse is to die for."

"Okay," I give in.

"We can have it back at my place."

My eyes widen at the thought. "Your place?"

"Yes, that is if you want to come over for a nightcap. We can have some coffee and dessert."

"And that's it?"

"I'm nothing if not a gentleman, Ellie," Aiden says with a wink.

Oh, yeah, right, I smile.

I know exactly what kind of gentleman he is.

I've seen some of his work in the bedroom.

But that just makes me even more excited about going to his apartment.

———

AIDEN PULLS over to the valet in front of his Park Avenue apartment building.

After tipping the valet, he says hello to the doorman who holds the door for us and welcomes us inside.

The foyer has all the charm of a pre-war

building, but also all the amenities of a contemporary apartment building. There's 24-hour concierge and staff service, a fine dining restaurant, housekeeping on demand, and a fitness center.

Aiden's apartment is on the twenty-fourth floor of Emery Roths fabled Ritz Tower, high above Park Avenue.

Once he shows me inside, the first thing I notice is how pin-drop quiet it is. None of the noise of the city below penetrates inside.

It's so quiet that it sounds as if we are somewhere in the country, miles away from Manhattan. My heels make a loud clicking sound as we walk along the herringbone hardwood floors.

Looking up, I see thick crown moldings and soaring twelve-foot ceilings throughout.

The elegant foyer welcomes me to this sophisticated home, leading to the sprawling and sun-filled corner living room, which features five oversized windows.

We walk past the state-of-the-art kitchen with custom cabinetry, marble countertops and backsplash, and beautiful stainless steel appliances.

"Do you cook often?" I ask.

He shrugs. "Not as much as I would like."

Hmm, a lover who also likes to cook? I could

definitely get used to that.

"I can't even make scrambled eggs," I confess.

"Well, we'll have to remedy that, won't we?"

Aiden opens a cabinet, which I thought was the pantry, but is actually a large wine cellar.

He takes a few moments to decide on the particular wine that he wants.

"Before we have that, can I have a tour of the rest of the house?" I ask.

"Of course."

Aiden leads me down a private corridor toward the bedrooms.

The master suite faces west over the Park and features a spacious and windowed marble bath and walk-in closet and the other bedroom also contains an en suite.

The third bedroom is just off the living room and is a large library with built-in oak bookcases.

"You have a beautiful home," I say when we get back to the living room.

I look out of the floor-to-ceiling window onto the city below. It's hard to imagine that a bachelor lives here.

"Thank you," Aiden says, taking a step closer to me. I can feel his breath on my neck, and it sends shivers up my spine.

Putting his arm around my lower back, he turns me around to face him.

His eyes turn a deeper shade without giving up the innocent and mysterious quality that drew me to them in the first place.

Suddenly, he reaches out and brushes his fingers along my bottom lip. His fingertips feel both rough and soft at the same time. He leans closer to me and I feel him breathing in and out on my face. I lick my lips in anticipation.

Aiden buries his fingers in my hair and tilts my head slightly to the side. It's about to happen. I close my eyes and wait for our lips to touch.

His lips are soft, almost effervescent. He tilts my head back and drops his. His tongue feels foreign and familiar at the same time.

His kisses are so soft and slow that the hair on the back of my neck stands up with each touch. Slowly, his lips make their way away from my lips and onto my neck.

Aiden's hands run down my back and then come back to my shoulders.

He presses his hard body against mine.

Our legs touch, sending shivers through me. I open my legs a little wider and he pushes himself even closer to me. A moment later, we intertwine as one.

"Aiden, wait," I whisper.

"What's wrong?" He pulls away from me and looks into my eyes.

When his hair falls into his face, it touches my forehead and it feels like little butterfly kisses.

"No, nothing." I shake my head.

I don't even know what I'm thinking. I don't really want to stop. I'm just having trouble losing myself in the moment.

If I let this happen, what does it mean?

Where do we stand?

Suddenly, a million contradictory thoughts rush through my mind.

Aiden continues to kiss my lips and neck, but not going any further without my saying so. I can feel him waiting for my permission.

You need to get it together, Ellie, I say silently to myself.

You want this.

You want him.

And as for the future?

Who the hell ever knows what the future holds?

In between our kisses, I look up into Aiden's eyes.

Even though this strong, alpha male doesn't

seem like the type, he makes me feel incredibly safe and comfortable.

A big part of me feels like I've known him my whole life. Like we should've been together way before this weekend.

It's as if we belong together.

"It doesn't feel like I've just met you," I finally say.

"Really?"

"Yeah, I don't know what it is. I just feel like I've known you my whole life."

He smiles and licks his lips. The twinkle in his eyes makes him look like his old mischievous self.

"Okay, fine, laugh at me," I say. The smile quickly disappears.

"Oh, I'm not. I'm smiling because I agree with you," he says with all seriousness.

"You do?"

"I'm falling for you, Ellie," he says quietly. We stare into each other's eyes until we see each other's souls.

"I feel like I'm falling for you, too," I say after a moment.

Aiden tilts my neck back and kisses me. A minute later, he pulls away, grabs my hand, and leads me to the bedroom.

The lights in the bedroom are dimmed low and he pauses for a second at the foot of the bed.

"Why are you looking at me like that?" I ask.

"Because you're the most beautiful woman I've ever seen," Aiden whispers without missing a beat. I blush and turn away. Now that can't be true, can it?

"No, you have to believe me," he says.

"Why?"

"Because it's the truth," he says. "I know you don't believe me. But I wish that you would. I wish you could see yourself from my eyes."

I look up at him and see a gaze of adoration staring back at me.

He really does think that I'm the most beautiful woman he's ever seen.

The confidence in his voice is disarming, and I can't help but blush again.

Aiden leans over and kisses me again. Unlike before, his lips are now more forceful, more powerful. As he presses his body into mine, all I feel is the hardness of his muscles.

His kisses become harder and begin to border on pain, but the good kind.

The kind that sends shivers through your body. As I push back at him, I feel him rise a little above me and with one swift motion he tosses me onto the bed.

After he lowers himself on top of me, our bodies begin to move as one. Through his pants, I can feel the girth and the substantial size of his cock.

I want to see it and feel it in my hand.

I need to taste it.

His hands make their way down my body with expert precision.

Quickly, I regret the fact that I wore jeans.

Unlike a short dress, which would be near my waist right about now, jeans, especially tight jeans, require a lot more maneuvering.

But they don't faze Aiden one bit.

He unbuttons the top button, flashing me a smile, and then pulls down the zipper with his teeth. I blush again, but wait in anticipation as he sits up and pulls my jeans off me.

Once my legs are freed, Aiden slides his hands back up, across the curves of my hips and up my hipbones. He stops briefly around my belly button, teasing me and making me even more wet.

Suddenly, he kisses me lightly around my belly button and then runs his tongue down to the top of my panties.

My body rises and falls with each kiss.

I pull my legs closed to try to stop myself from getting even more aroused, without much avail.

As Aiden continues to tease me, by kissing me along my panty line, my mouth suddenly dries up of all moisture and feels as parched as a desert.

When he returns his gaze to my eyes, I can see that he's planning something.

A moment later, I realize that he has his mind set on pulling off my blouse. I give in immediately.

Along with my blouse, he unclips my bra, letting my erect nipples fall nearly into his mouth.

"Wow," he whispers, placing the tip of my nipple into his mouth and sucking on it lightly.

"Your breasts...wow, Ellie. Just wow," Aiden says, sharing his time between my breasts.

I lie back down and indulge in the moment.

"I love the way you say my name," I confess.

"Oh, you do?"

"Yes. And I want to hear you say it when you cum."

OMG, did I really just say that?

I've relaxed a bit too much.

I can't believe that I let that slip.

That's not something I should say, or anyone should say, out loud. But it just makes Aiden chuckle.

"I will as long as you promise to scream my name when I make you cum."

I stare at him, dumbfounded, having lost all ability to speak.

A part of me wants to die of embarrassment, and another part wants to wrap my legs around him and force him inside of me.

Aiden pulls off his pants and briefs, exposing his large and very sexy member.

It's tan just like the rest of his body and straight.

He climbs on top of me and I wrap my hands around his strong, toned butt. The skin of his butt is soft and delicate, but the bulging muscles underneath are powerful.

My legs fall open for him and he grinds on me for a few moments. There's only a thin layer of lace panties separating us and I want him so much that I wish he would just tear them off me as soon as possible.

A moment later, as if he had read my mind, he jumps up and pulls my panties off, tossing them onto the floor.

The area in between my legs is begging for him. I don't think I've ever been so wet before.

"I want you," Aiden whispers, pushing himself inside of me. I let out a moan of pleasure.

"I want you, too," I whisper when I regain the ability to speak.

His motions in and out of me are elegant and powerful. Quickly, we begin to move as one as he moves deeper and deeper inside of me.

A few moments later, my legs start to feel numb and I know that I'm getting close. I point my toes as my body seizes up. A soothing sensation starts to fill my entire body and I get closer and closer to that blissful release.

"Oh my God, Aiden!" I moan loudly. As soon as he hears me, he starts to move faster and faster, driving me wild.

"Aiden!" I scream as our movements speed up and then a warm sensation pulses through my whole body. I give up and give in and let go of myself completely.

"Ellie!" he screams, a few moments after my body goes limp under him.

"Ellie!" he screams again and again into my ear, moving his hips faster and faster.

"Aiden," I whisper when I finally come back to my senses.

"Ellie," he whispers one last time, collapsing on top of me.

CHAPTER 27 - ELLIE

WHAT HAPPENS AFTERWARD…

L ying in bed after making love to Aiden makes me feel alive and invigorated.

It's almost like I have been asleep for a long time and I'm just waking up.

I glance over at Aiden and the way the covers cradle his toned torso, making him look even more tan and sexy.

"Ellie, are you staring at me?" Aiden asks, keeping his eyes closed.

"Yes," I say, pulling lightly at the covers. They easily slip off his manhood, exposing all the yummy bits.

"I need a break, honey," he mumbles. "You wore me out."

I laugh.

While I feel full of energy, the evening's activities have clearly drained Aiden of his.

After a few moments, he opens his eyes and gives me one of those looks that pierces through my very soul.

If I weren't already naked, I'd feel completely naked. Exposed.

Yet, the feeling is not threatening in the least.

I feel safe with him.

Safe and well-taken care of.

"Since you don't seem to be the least bit tired," Aiden says, turning toward me and propping his head up with his hand. "Why don't we talk?"

"I like the sound of that," I say. "So, where are you from? What's your family like?"

The expression on his face tells me that he was not ready for my quick fire questions, but these things have been on my mind ever since we met. I mean, I hardly know two things about him.

"I guess you didn't google me yet."

"No, I did," I say. "But you know, newspaper articles. They're often full of falsehoods. Plus, I want to hear it from you."

"Okay...well, I grew up in a pretty average family. My parents fought a lot, but refused to get divorced. I think they couldn't really afford to live apart, so they stayed together and made everyone's life miserable."

"Oh, I'm sorry," I say.

"It's okay. I'm way over it. My way of dealing with it was just to spend all of my time tinkering with computers."

"Where did you grow up?"

"Near Boston. My mom was a nurse at a hospital, she often worked the night shift. My dad was a garbage man. He didn't work much during the day, so he spent most of his free time drinking."

"I'm so sorry."

He shrugs and looks away. "They loved me in their own way, I know that. But I knew from a young age that the only way I wasn't going to have the same life that they had was to study hard and go to college."

"That's why you went to Yale?"

"Yep. It was my dream school, actually. And I still feel bad about dropping out to start Owl."

"Even though you're the founder of Owl and it's such a huge company now?"

"Yeah, even so," he says. "Just thinking back, I don't think it would've made much of a difference if I had just finished my degree, you know? I mean, what's a year in the long scheme of things?"

I've never thought of that myself. As much as I had enjoyed my college experience, I'm not sure if I'd be for expanding it for another year.

"How was college for you?" he asks.

"It was fun. It had its hard parts. But mostly, it was a blast. Also, very different from the real world."

"Tell me about it."

"I guess that's what I liked about it most. It just felt like this layover between high school and adulthood. I mean, we are adults, but we're not expected to be adults. Not in any real way. I just think about all of those people who don't go to college and just go straight to work. Or have kids at a young age. I really admire them because I definitely couldn't do that. There was no way that I would be ready for any of that now, let alone when I was eighteen."

Aiden nods in agreement.

Neither of us say anything for a few moments and then another thought pops into my head.

"So, what about your marriage?" I ask.

"What do you want to know?"

"What was it like? To get married so young, I mean?" I ask.

"I don't know what came over me. I guess I was just in love. She was my first real girlfriend and I remember really wanting to marry her. Her parents were not pleased over the city hall wedding and things went awry after that. She said we rushed into it and she couldn't really live with herself over it."

"Did you know her from high school?" I ask.

"No." Aiden shakes his head. "She was from an old family from Ohio."

"Well, you know all families are basically the same age. There's no such thing as an old family. Some just keep better records," I joke. He forces a smile.

"Unlike my family, hers was very prominent in the community. They owned one of the biggest houses in the state. And back then, I never had much money."

I know a little bit about old money.

No matter how much money you have now, they are not the types to welcome new money with open arms.

"I think what I'm trying to say is that we were from two different worlds and her family never accepted me. I guess she lost her mind momentarily by marrying me, but then regained it when we got a divorce."

Suddenly, I feel a pang in my chest.

"It sounds like you still have feelings for her," I say.

"No, I don't, not at all," he says quickly. "We were just very good friends and very close, and I guess a part of me still misses that friendship."

I nod, feeling a bit relieved.

Actually, I know exactly what he means.

That's pretty much how I feel toward Tom.

"And after her?" I ask.

"What do you mean?"

"Any significant relationships?"

"No, after my marriage, I've been pretty settled into the life of a bachelor."

"Yes, I saw that online. Lots of models and actresses," I say.

I try not to sound jealous, but I can't really.

I am jealous.

Even if they are in his past. Of course, I have no way of knowing that for sure. I mean, are they really in his past?

"But no one special?"

"Not until you," Aiden says, moving a strand of hair out of my eyes.

"What?" I sit up in bed.

"I just feel different toward you, Ellie. Different than I ever felt before. And I'm not the type to tell women that. In fact, most of the time I feel absolutely nothing for the women I spend time with. And then you came along...and changed all that."

I can't help but blush. I turn my face away from him to hide my red cheeks.

"You're just so beautiful, Ellie." He pulls me closer to him and kisses me on the lips.

"Now, it's your turn," he says. "Tell me something you never told anyone before."

I try to think of something that I've never shared with anyone. The thing is that I'm not a girl with too many secrets. I wish I were more mysterious, but I'm not.

"I like the games you play," I say after a moment. "I've never been tied up before, but it felt really good. It just made me feel so free, in a way."

"Really?" Aiden smiles. "That's exciting."

"Yes. Exciting and scary. I mean, I'm completely immobile and yet there's something very liberating about it. I don't know what."

"I don't know either," he says. "But I'm glad you're enjoying it."

"How about you?" I ask.

"You mean you want me to tell you something I've never told anyone?"

I nod.

"I'm afraid that if I ever stop working I'm going to be poor again. Poor like I was growing up. I mean my parents had a two bedroom house but then they lost it, and that's when we started going back and forth between various rental houses. I was always worried about where we would live next. Angry landlords were always knocking on our door because my parents weren't paying the rent, threatening to kick us out. My mom said they were idle threats, but they weren't all the time. We got evicted a few times and had to live on people's couches."

"Oh, I'm so sorry."

"I never told anyone that before, Ellie."

"Thank you for telling me."

"And despite all of my money, I'm still afraid that I'll be back there again. Not having enough money to eat or pay for the roof over my head."

"Well, the roof that you have over your head now does cost a pretty penny," I joke. He smiles.

"But, seriously, I'm sorry about that," I add. "I mean, you went through a lot as a kid and it must've been really scary to get evicted."

"One day we had this truck pull up to our apartment building and they came in and repossessed all of our furniture and the television. Apparently, my mom didn't pay the rental people so they just took it all back. I had to sleep on the floor with my pillow and blanket."

I shake my head.

I don't know what to say.

I wrap my arms around him and tell him that it's all going to be okay.

That I'm here for him, and still that doesn't seem like enough.

We fall asleep in each other's arms and only awake when the sun is streaming in through the window.

When I open my eyes, I see Aiden standing dressed in his impeccable suit in front of me.

"I'm sorry, but I have to go to work," he says, giving me a kiss on the forehead.

"Oh, okay," I mumble sleepily.

"I was just wondering. Would you like to be mine for a week again?" Aiden asks. "I promise no sex clubs this time."

A smile forms on my lips before I even have the chance to reply.

"Is that a yes?"

"Yes, sir, Mr. Black."

CHAPTER 28 - ELLIE

WHEN I'M SURPRISED TWICE...

I spend the morning wandering around Central Park.

It's a beautiful crisp fall day and the leaves are just turning shades of gold.

I love the crunchy sound they make under my feet as I walk. It's still warm, in the low 60's, so I take the opportunity to sit down on the bench and people watch for a bit.

It's amazing how much time there is in the day when you don't have to go to work.

Now, there seems to be time for almost anything.

Day dreaming.

Reading.

Walking around in the park.

Just grabbing a cup of coffee without rushing somewhere.

My job didn't feel particularly stressful, but now that I'm no longer working there, it definitely feels like a weight has dropped off my shoulders.

"Ellie?" a familiar voice asks, tapping me on my shoulder. I turn around and come face-to-face with Tom.

"Hey." I smile.

"What are you doing here?"

"Um, nothing really. Just relaxing. Enjoying the day. And you?"

"Same." He shrugs. "I took a day off. I need some time."

He slouches a bit and looks down at the ground.

I know Tom well enough to know that he's waiting for me to ask him why.

But I don't want to indulge. I don't want to see him actually, and I'm a bit peeved that he's here interrupting my alone time.

Without an invitation, he sits down next to me on the bench. I decide not to indulge him.

Instead, I turn my attention to the Kindle app on my phone.

"What are you reading?" he asks after a few moments of silence.

"You wouldn't like it," I say.

"And how do you know that?"

"Because you think romance novels are trashy."

"No, c'mon tell me," he insists.

"It's a billionaire romance with steamy sex scenes," I say.

"Hmm. Is the girl the billionaire or the guy?"

"The guy."

"How original," Tom says sarcastically.

"Listen, I didn't ask for your opinion, did I? The sex is hot and the writing is fast paced. It's a nice way to unwind."

Tom nods without really agreeing.

I'm about to ask him to leave when my phone rings. It's Aiden.

"Hey." I pick up the phone.

"Hey, stranger," Aiden says. "I have a surprise for you. Tonight."

"Tonight?"

"I'm sending a package over to your place now with a courier."

"A present?" I ask. "For me?"

"Yes. Hope to see you in it tonight."

"Will you pick me up?"

"No, the directions where I want you to meet me will be in the package," he says.

"Can't wait."

When I hang up, my heart is still fluttering a bit, but then I look over at Tom. The sour expression on his face tells me everything I want to know.

"Who was that?"

"Nobody."

"Nobody?"

"It's just a guy I'm seeing. It's none of your business," I say, standing up. "Listen, I have to get back home. I have some work to do."

"What work? You're unemployed." He chuckles.

"You know, I don't know how I didn't notice this before. You can be such an asshole sometimes."

————

WHEN I GET HOME, the package from Aiden is waiting for me with the doorman.

It's a big white box with a pink bow around it.

I take it up to our apartment and unwrap it as soon as I enter the foyer. Inside, I find an exquisite short black sleeveless dress. I don't know what it's made of it, but the material definitely feels luxurious and very expensive.

When I put it on, I feel like a princess.

I twirl around the living room and watch as the fabric rises and falls with me.

Since it's a little black dress, almost any shoe goes with it. So I reach for my $100 DSW pair of black pumps.

Unlike Caroline, I do not have an expensive shoe habit.

I arrive at the bar in mid-town promptly at eight. It's an upscale bar where everyone is dressed in suits and ties and dresses.

I've never been here before and, at first, I'm a bit apprehensive about grabbing a seat at the bar by myself.

I've never really sat at the bar by myself before because it's the prime location for all sorts of creeps to hit on you.

But this time, I decide to be brave.

Besides, Aiden is going to be here soon, right?

I take a seat at the far end of the bar and order a mojito. While I'm waiting, Aiden comes up to me and kisses me behind the ear.

"Hey there, stranger."

"Oh, hey!" I say and give him a brief hug. He takes the seat next to me and orders an Old Fashioned.

"Thank you so much for the dress."

"No, thank you for wearing it. You look gorgeous in it."

"How is it that you can pick out clothes for me so easily? I mean, when I find a dress I like at the store, I have to try on a few different sizes before I find the one that fits right. And yet, you're two for two."

"Ah, it's a skill, I guess," he says, nodding to the bartender when his drink is ready.

"No, seriously, I want to know."

"Seriously? Seriously, I have a buyer. She saw what you look like, and she has an expert eye for these things."

I take a sip of my mojito when it arrives. It's incredibly fresh and the combination of acid and sugar on my tongue makes me salivate and crave it more and more.

For a few minutes, we lose ourselves in our conversation and in each other's eyes. Everything he says makes perfect sense to me and I agree with it wholeheartedly.

And everything I say resonates with him as well. There's no other way to describe this moment other than that we are completely in-sync.

"Well, hello there." I hear an unfamiliar female voice behind me.

When I turn around, I see a tall woman with

razor sharp cheekbones and a razor-sharp aggressive haircut. Don't get me wrong.

She's gorgeous. But the way her eyes flicker when she speaks makes my stomach turn in fear.

"Alexis, what are you doing here?" Aiden asks. The shocked expression on his face convinces me that this is not a planned surprise.

"Your secretary said you would be here."

"Why are you even asking her about me?" He demands to know. "Can't you see that I'm on a date?"

"I'm asking about you because you're my husband."

"Ex-husband. Of many years mind you. Why don't you talk to your present-day husband about whatever it is you're bothering me with?"

Suddenly, the expression on Alexis's face changes. The hardness vanishes as tears start to roll down her cheeks.

"Aiden, I'm so, so sorry. I just didn't know who else to turn to. You know that I don't have any friends except for you. And I really needed to talk to you."

Aiden shakes his head like he has heard this before, but doesn't ask her to leave.

"The thing is that he left. He just took off on Rory and me. Can you believe that? I mean, I haven't heard from him in a week. And I haven't been sleeping again. And I really need a sleeping pill again."

"No, Alexis! No. Absolutely not. You cannot not take any pills. You're an addict. Do you want to go to rehab again?"

"No," Alexis sobs, wiping her eyes with my napkin. When the spot next to Aiden opens up, she gladly takes the seat.

"No, you're not sitting down, Alexis," Aiden says sternly. "I'm on a date."

"I know. But I don't know where Tyler is; do you know what that's like? I mean he might be dead."

"Tyler's not dead, Alexis. He's probably in Vegas gambling away Rory's college fund."

Alexis drops her head and continues to sob. Suddenly, I feel like a third wheel.

"I'm going to go," I whisper to Aiden and get up.

He tries to stop me, but I brush him off and walk away. Whatever is going on in there is none of my business.

She clearly needs him and I don't want to feel like an uninvited guest on my own date.

But Aiden doesn't let me get away that easily. He catches up with me halfway down the street.

"No, you're not leaving," he says defiantly. "She has taken up enough of my life already."

"But she's your ex and your friend."

"I don't care. You don't know her, Ellie. Alexis is the type of woman to have drama piled on drama. Her life is always in ruins and ready for someone else to save. Well, I can't be that person anymore. Please, just wait for a second. I'm going to put her in a cab and send her home. I'm not dealing with her tonight."

CHAPTER 29 - ELLIE

WHEN SHE FINALLY LEAVES...

I can't lie, a big part of me was curious about what Alexis was like when Aiden first told me about her. But now that I've seen her...I was not expecting her to be quite that drop dead gorgeous.

Standing outside the bar, I still can't believe that she actually crashed our date.

And what about that assistant of Aiden's?

Did she really tell her where we were?

It has been years since they were married and yet...the relationship between the two of them seems way too close. I want to leave and go home, but Aiden urges me to stay.

He convinces me with his 'please'. I wait as

Aiden cuts his conversation with Alexis short and puts her into a cab.

When he comes back to me, he invites me back inside. But that place has been soured. Now, all I can think about is his ex-wife and how long her legs are in comparison to mine.

"I'm so, so sorry about that," Aiden says. "You have to believe me. We are completely through."

"So, why does she still come around? I thought she lived in Ohio. Why is she acting like you're not?"

A cold gust of wind blows and I regret the fact that I didn't bring a coat. These warm summer nights are quickly fading into autumn.

"No, she lives in New York now with her husband and kid. Her parents are paying for their apartment. The thing is that Alexis has a lot of issues. After we broke up, she got pregnant right away with her high school boyfriend's baby. They got married because her parents insisted on it and their marriage hasn't been good for anyone involved, including the baby. She was in a bad car accident a few years back and got hooked on pain pills and has been in and out of rehab ever since."

"But what does any of this have to do with you?" I ask. Aiden takes off his jacket and puts it around my shoulders. It's hot from his body heat and I revel in its warmth.

"Frankly, I don't know." He shrugs. "Except that somehow we became friends again over the years and I was always there for her through her rehabs and her issues. I was the one person who she could turn to."

"Did you two...ever get back together?" I ask, carefully choosing my words. First loves are difficult to get over and tend to stick with people for life. And that doesn't even count those who have been married.

"No." Aiden shakes his head. "Absolutely not. I was over her even before we officially got divorced, Ellie. She's just this complicated aspect of my life who is still there. I'm a friend. I care about her daughter. I want her to get better and find a better man. But I do not, and I mean it, I do not want that man to be me."

Aiden looks straight into my eyes as he says that. There's certainty in the tone of his voice and in the conviction with which he speaks and that makes me feel relieved. He is telling the truth. I know it.

"If you don't want to go back to the bar, will you come over for a nightcap?" Aiden asks.

"Doesn't a nightcap usually take place at the end of the night?" I ask, flashing him a smile.

"Well, tonight was nothing if not exciting, wouldn't you say?"

———

ON THE SECOND visit to his beautiful apartment, I notice all the details that I've missed before. The exquisite banister, the gorgeous crown molding, the beautiful window frames around the floor-to-ceiling windows lining his living room.

There are also books everywhere. Besides the vast library, there are books on practically every end table and console table. Much to my surprise, a number of them are novels.

"Have you read this one?" He points to *A Widow for One Year* by John Irving.

"Actually, John Irving is one of my favorite authors," I say. "Have you read his latest, In One Person?"

"Yes, I have. It's exquisite," he says, running his fingers along my forearm as I thumb through *A Widow for One Year*. "What kind of books do you read?"

"All kinds actually. I like Irving, but I also like

Jane Austen and Charles Dickens. And Anne Rice, and E. L. James, and Sylvia Day."

He smiles coyly.

"What? You don't think some of those fit in with the rest?"

"Oh, no, not at all." He shakes his head. "I love reading all sorts of books. But given how I like to spend the nights, I have a real taste for romance as well. More than your typical guy."

"I'd say that," I agree. "Most don't come anywhere near fiction, let alone romance. And the ones that do like to read fiction tend to end their education with Hemingway."

"Oh, but there're so many amazing stories out there. I mean, what about Marquez, and De Sade, and Isabel Allende? Though I can enjoy a traditional male narrative yarn like those spun by Jim Harrison as well."

I shake my head in amazement.

The authors he had just listed were my favorites as well. But after so many years of disappointment, I gave up on trying to convince my literary-inclined friends at Yale about the merits of Danielle Steel, E. L. James, and Stephanie Meyer, they allowed their snobbish attitudes to keep them away from fun and enticing contemporary fiction.

And yet, here was this man, who actually got me. It's like he understood where I was coming from on this innate level that I hadn't even shared with him yet.

He got me because he felt the same way.

"I just don't think we need to create these boxes between literary and popular fiction. I think it's all about the goal of the book. Popular fiction is there to entertain and allow you to escape while literary fiction is there to challenge your thinking and show you a different perspective.

Of course, the holy grail of any writer is to create a piece of work that's both challenging and important, as well as relevant and popular. And if you ask a million critics about what that book is they'll have a million different opinions. Mainly because what's relevant and entertaining to one person tends to be something different for another."

I reach up and press my lips against his.

I can't help it.

When you hear someone say exactly what you're thinking but in a way that's way better than you could ever conceptualize in your mind, you just have to show him what that means to you.

"What's that for?" Aiden asks.

"You're just amazing, do you know that?" I ask.

"I don't know. I think you'll have to show me."

"I'd love to," I say.

"Oh, really?" Aiden raises his eyebrows. "Well, in that case, I have a surprise for you."

He grabs my hand and leads me to the master bedroom. There, in the middle of the room, right in front of his spacious bed, I see a swing.

"What's that?" I ask, walking over and tugging on it. It's attached to the ceiling and the swing itself is made of a soft but sturdy fabric, which feels a bit like silk.

"This wasn't here before," I say.

"No, it wasn't." He shakes his head. "I only take it out for special occasions. Like tonight."

"Hmm," I say, licking my lips. I don't know how it works but I would be lying if I said I wasn't excited to find out.

"Do you think you want to take it for a spin?" Aiden asks.

I think about it for a moment. "Yes, I would, Mr. Black."

A serious expression comes over his face. He spins me around and unzips my dress.

I like the force and the power with which he works. It feels like I'm almost a rag doll under his strong hands and I love being a rag doll.

He slips the dress down, leaving me in a strapless bra and panties. Then he puts my hands up in the air and ties them to the top of the swing.

The restraints are soft but strong. I tug on them but I can't break free.

"You've been a bad girl, Ellie," Aiden says with all seriousness. Suddenly, he is completely within the character of Mr. Black, the man I met what seems like a century ago on his yacht. While Aiden is complicated and multi-textured, Mr. Black is not. He has razor-sharp focus on one thing - pleasure - and that's what I crave most about him.

"Yes, I have," I say.

"Yes, you have, what?" Mr. Black asks.

"Yes, I have been a bad girl, sir," I correct myself.

I've always thought it was a little cheesy when I heard or read about women calling men sir in the sexual context, but something about it is ridiculously hot.

I've given him control. He's in charge, at least in this moment. There's something completely freeing about it.

"That's better."

"Now, what am I going to do with you?" Mr. Black asks, walking around me and staring at my body.

My heart skips a beat as I wait on his decision. Slowly, he undoes my bra and pulls down my panties. Then he bends down and puts one of my breasts into his mouth. He squeezes lightly and I feel a little shock of electricity rush through my body.

While flicking my nipples with his tongue, he reaches in between my legs and pushes them apart. Then he sticks his finger deep within me and starts to massage me. My clit begins to throb.

I've never had anyone touch me like this while I was standing up and the feeling is overwhelming.

A few moments later, he presses something against my inner thigh. It's a small vibrator, which he expertly maneuvers right onto my clit while pushing his fingers deep inside of me and not taking his mouth off my breasts. I start to moan immediately.

Not being able to move my hands, and being forced to experience pleasure in such a restrained environment, makes my whole body pulsate with feeling.

My calves start to cramp up and a warm soothing sensation from deep inside is about to erupt to the surface.

"Oh, no, sweetie," Mr. Black says, pulling away from me and slowing down. "You can't orgasm so easily. What would be the fun in that?"

"I can't?" I plead. "But I want to. I really, really want to."

"Oh, I know, sweetie. But you didn't call me sir. And you haven't been teased enough quite yet."

I let out a little sigh as he presses the vibrator deep within me and my whole body starts to shake with pleasure.

"Okay, I'm going to try something a little different now. Let's see how you like it."

Mr. Black walks around and ties the loose ends of the fabric around my breasts and torso. He puts my arms behind my back and ties them behind as well.

Then he drops me to the floor and ties the other loose ends of the swing around the upper part of my thighs, bending my legs back and tying my ankles to my thighs.

Finally, he ties all parts of me together, connecting my thighs to my ankles to my torso.

"Now, I'm going to pull you up until you're parallel to the floor. Does that sound good?"

"Yes, sir." I nod, my body shivering in anticipation.

Mr. Black pulls up and, within a moment, I'm suspended in mid-air completely parallel to the floor. My legs are wide open and my pussy is completely exposed.

He spins me a little to get me just in the place that he wants me. Then he takes his fingers and presses them deep inside of me. When he moves them around a bit, I feel myself get completely wet.

"Oh my God," I moan in pleasure.

I hear him kneel down somewhere behind me and press his lips to me.

His tongue runs up and around my clit and then makes its way deep inside of me.

The sensation is unlike anything I've ever experienced before.

The weightlessness that's provided by the swing exposes and concentrates all attention on my pleasure center, making me give off moans unlike the kind I've ever given off before.

A few moments later, Mr. Black swings me away from him and then back toward him. I love how the air feels as I push it out of my way with my body.

On one of the times that I come back toward him, he enters me, sending my body into overdrive. Mr. Black holds onto the swing as he pushes in and out of me, filling me completely.

"Oh, Aiden," I moan.

"Do you want to cum?" he asks.

"Yes, I do. I really do, sir," I mumble.

There's no way I could stop the orgasm if I wanted to. A familiar soothing sensation starts to pulsate through my body as I let myself go completely.

"Ellie!" Mr. Black screams a few moments later as he pounds into me over and over.

I feel myself closing in around his large cock, taking him deep within me. I want to stay in this moment forever.

CHAPTER 30 - ELLIE

WHEN ANOTHER INVITATION ARRIVES...

The following day, I spend feverishly writing about how my unassuming main character gets auctioned off at a fancy yacht party to a very hot and wealthy eligible bachelor.

I find myself writing so fast that I can barely keep up with my own thoughts. Somewhere in the middle of the auction scene, it hits me.

I can't wait to get to the good, juicy parts where they finally have sex. Just like everything else in the story, I still want to tell the truth when I write about what happens between my protagonist and her mysterious stranger.

Why?

Because the truth of what happened that night is

more exciting and arousing than anything else I could make up.

Of course, writing that first sex scene makes my mind go back to my own experience in the swing from just yesterday. It has been twenty-four hours since Mr. Black turned my world upside down and I've only just begun processing a little bit of what happened.

The swing was quite a surprise, but the pleasure it provided was even more of a surprise. The constraints and restraints that I experienced, just being tied to the bed, was nothing like what I experienced last night - being suspended in air with my legs spread open for him to do with what he liked.

And I liked, no loved, everything he did to me.

Suddenly, a knock at the door breaks my concentration.

"Oh my God, are you still working?" Caroline asks, rolling her eyes. "I swear, ever since you quit your job, you seem to be working 24/7."

That's not entirely untrue.

Ever since I quit a job I hated and started doing something I loved, work doesn't really feel like work anymore. I actually wake up looking forward to writing.

"Listen, will you take a break for a second? There's a package out there for you."

I follow her into the kitchen.

She hands me a bland Amazon looking package and I search my mind trying to remember the last thing I ordered from there.

That's the nice thing about Amazon, isn't it?

You order something and then forget about it completely. And when it arrives, a few days later, it's like a little surprise.

When I open the nondescript cardboard box, I find another smaller box inside. It looks familiar.

It's gold plated just like the one Caroline got before, with whimsical twirls around the edges.

Except this time, instead of Caroline's name, I see my name. Underneath my engraved name is tomorrow's date. Eight p.m.

The box has the same elegant knob with the same custom monogram inside made of foil in gold on silk emblazoned on the inside of the flap cover.

"Oh my God, oh my God!" Caroline squeals with excitement. "Is this another invitation to a yacht party?"

"Looks like it."

I look over the invitation once again, a little bit confused.

Is this from Aiden?

Is he having another party?

Will there be another auction?

It's not that I expected him to stop hosting parties.

I mean, parties have to be planned ahead of time and I'm sure this one was on the calendar way before we met.

But why the hell am I getting another invitation?

"Oh my God! You have to take me. I took you!" Caroline demands.

"You want to go?" I ask. "But you didn't even have a good time before. You didn't want anything to do with that auction."

"I know, I know." She waves her hand at me. "But the thing is that I sort of regret it. I mean, you had fun. You met Aiden. Maybe I can meet someone."

I shake my head.

I don't really know how to wrap my mind around this.

So, I do the only thing I can think of.

I dial Aiden's number. When he picks up, I ask him about the party.

"I invited you because I thought we would have fun again. The party has been planned for months," he says nonchalantly. I'm having a hard time reading him.

"So, will there be an auction again?" I whisper into the phone. I don't really know why I'm whispering.

Caroline knows all about it, but I still feel a little timid about the whole thing.

"Well, you'll have to come to find out," he says cryptically. "Listen, I'm in the middle of a meeting. I can't talk now. See you tomorrow."

He's just assuming that I'm going to come, but honestly I'm not sure. I mean, what's the point?

I don't want to participate in another auction that's for sure. I don't want some other man to get me.

I just want to be with Aiden. And until I got this invitation, I thought that he just wanted to be with me, too.

Suddenly, my phone rings again.

"Hey, it's me again," Aiden says. "I didn't think I ended that conversation very well. I'm sorry."

"It's fine," I mumble.

"No, let me explain. I'm having another party. Yes, that's true. And you got an invitation because I really want you to come. And I mean really. I don't want to be with anyone else. And I think we would have fun there."

I think about that for a moment.

"Please come. It's just going to be an over the top, elegant, crazy affair just like last time. And it wouldn't be the same without you."

"You really want me there?" I ask.

"Yes."

"Why?"

"Because I'm falling for you. And I've never felt this way about anyone before."

My heart skips a beat. "I'm falling for you, too," I whisper.

When I hang up, I turn around to face Caroline.

"Oh my god, we're going, right? This means we're going?" she asks, jumping up and down.

A small smile comes over my face.

"Yes, yes, yes!" she squeals at the top of her lungs, grabbing me by the shoulders.

"Okay, okay." I push her away. "Yes, we're going."

CAN'T WAIT to read more? Find out what happens to Ellie when she goes back to the yacht... **One-click BLACK RULES now!**

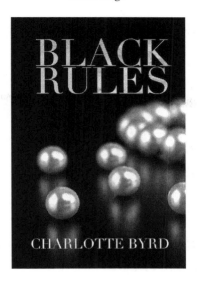

We don't belong together.

I should have never seen him again after our first night together. But I crave him.

I'm addicted to him. **He is my dark pleasure.**

Mr. Black is Aiden. Aiden is Mr. Black. Two sides of the same person.

Aiden is kind and sweet. **Mr. Black is demanding** and rule-oriented.

When he invites me back to his yacht, I can't say no.

Another auction.

Another bid.

I'm supposed to be his. But then everything goes wrong....

One-click BLACK RULES Now!

SIGN UP for my **newsletter** to find out when I have new books!

You can also join my Facebook group, **Charlotte Byrd's Steamy Reads**, for exclusive giveaways and sneak peaks of future books.

I appreciate you sharing my books and telling your friends about them. Reviews help readers find my books! Please leave a review on your favorite site.

BOOKS BY CHARLOTTE BYRD

ebt series (can be read in any order)

DEBT

OFFER

UNKNOWN

WEALTH

ABOUT CHARLOTTE BYRD

*C*harlotte Byrd is the bestselling author of many contemporary romance novels. She lives in Southern California with her husband, son, and a crazy toy Australian Shepherd. She loves books, hot weather and crystal blue waters.

Write her here:

charlotte@charlotte-byrd.com

Check out her books here:

www.charlotte-byrd.com

Connect with her here:

www.facebook.com/charlottebyrdbooks

Instagram: @charlottebyrdbooks

Twitter: @ByrdAuthor

Facebook Group: Charlotte Byrd's Steamy Reads

Newsletter

COPYRIGHT

Printed in Great Britain
by Amazon